CHRISTMAS IN HIDING

CATE NOLAN

HARLEQUIN® LOVE INSPIRED® SUSPENSE

Recycling programs
for this product may
not exist in your area.

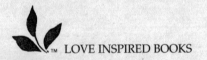

™ LOVE INSPIRED BOOKS

ISBN-13: 978-0-373-44701-5

Christmas in Hiding

Copyright © 2015 by Mary Curry

www.Harlequin.com

Printed in U.S.A.

For You are my hiding place; You protect me from trouble.
You surround me with songs of victory.
—Psalms 32:7

To my husband, who brought me roses
when I finished my first book.
Thank you for encouraging me through all the years since.

To my daughters, who have always been such a wondrous
source of love in my life. I am so proud of the women you
have become. Thank you for putting up with all the years
of Mommy's stories even when it must have been
a bit unnerving to help your mother plot murder.

To my parents and sisters,
who believed even when I didn't. Thank you for your love.

To all my friends at Seekerville, thank you for
your endless support and encouragement. You make this
road so much smoother and the ride much more fun.

A special thanks to Emily Rodmell for taking a chance on a
new author and offering so much of her wisdom in guiding
me through the Killer Voices contest and this story.

And finally, but always first, to my Lord
for His perfect timing. For making me wait
until I was writing what He called me to write
so I could more perfectly spread His message of love.

ONE

The Christmas party down the hall was making her head ache.

Callie Martin sank into a chair at the now-empty conference table and rested her head in her hands. She tried massaging her temples to alleviate the painful throb, but her hands were shaking too badly.

Drug conspiracy. Conspiracy to kidnap and murder. Money laundering conspiracy. Interstate travel in aid of drug trafficking. The assistant US attorney's litany echoed in her mind, clashing with the cheerful strains of "Jingle Bells."

In that other office, people were celebrating the season with food and music and good cheer. Callie didn't begrudge them their fun. Any other year she'd have been happy to join in. But their party was in such contrast to the meeting that had just ended in this room.

No Christmas cheer for her. No punch, no cookies. Only a throbbing headache as she sat alone in a sterile New York City office, terrified beyond imagining about what her future might hold.

Callie wrapped her arms around her torso and huddled into herself. When she'd entered the Federal Witness Security program in Texas, she'd thought she was testifying only about the murders she'd witnessed. But the meeting today had established a terrifying new reality. According to a very determined assistant US attorney, that nightmare moment in her life was only one small part of a much bigger scheme.

And they thought she knew something about it.

Callie couldn't sit still. She rose and started pacing the room. How could they think she knew more? She wasn't into drugs. She was a kindergarten teacher. She was supposed to be spending December knee-deep in glitter and tinsel, and helping her students with the nativity play.

Instead she was running for her life, hiding out in witness protection. No Christmas lights. No fake snow. No fancy cookies.

This had to be a mistake. A bad dream. She'd wake up, and Rick would still be alive and she'd... No. Not a bad dream. It was what her life had become.

She wanted Ben to come back upstairs. Ben Wilson had been her marshal, her protector, since the day she entered WITSEC. Earlier, after the assistant US attorney had laid all the accusations on the table, and the DEA agent had glared at her in disbelief for denying she knew anything, Ben had sensed her panic. Like the good handler he was, he'd tried to run interference, leaving her under guard while he escorted the attorney and the DEA agent to their cars.

Callie had no doubt he wanted to talk to them in private, but she didn't care. She'd just been grateful to see them leave. She'd blessed Ben for the solitude and the chance to gather her thoughts. But now she wanted him back. Wanted him to make sense of her world out of control.

"Jingle Bells" switched over to something softer, and Callie tried to calm herself. If only she could think straight. Understand what they wanted. She'd seen her ex-boyfriend and his band murdered. She'd told the authorities everything she knew. Every sordid detail of how that ex-boyfriend had turned out to be a drug dealer who was gunned down by the very people he worked with. She didn't know anything more than that.

Why didn't they believe her?

Distracted by her frantic thoughts, Callie almost missed the unfamiliar ring of her cell phone. Not many people called her on this new phone. Hope lifted her spirits as she noted Ben's name light up on the display, and she fumbled to grab the phone.

"Ben? Where are you? Did you talk to her? Did—"

His voice cut across her questions. "Another marshal... coming to get you." Erratic breathing punctuated the words, making them hard to understand. "His name... Jackson Walker. Go with him."

"What?" Ben had been her marshal from the start. Why go with someone else now?

"Don't go out front. Don't...even... Go... Leave New York."

Callie shook her head, trying to clear the confusion. This felt all wrong. The voice was so broken. Was it really even Ben? He'd been fine when he left. Did this have something to do with the meeting? Dread sucked her hope away. "What's going on? Why should I go with someone else?"

"Because your security has been compromised."

Callie swung around at the sound of the harsh voice behind her. A tall man blocked the doorway. Her first thought was he looked like someone she wouldn't want to meet in a dark alley. And she was supposed to go with him?

He flashed a badge at her. "Jackson Walker, US Marshals. Grab your purse and coat. We have to get out of here. Now."

Callie stared at the stranger. He didn't look like a marshal. His heavy jacket seemed straight out of an outdoors-man catalog, and he was wearing jeans and boots. The only thing missing was a cowboy hat. A dozen questions pinged in her brain. She settled on the most urgent. "How do I know I can trust you?"

He appeared to think about it for all of ten seconds. "You don't. But I'm all you've got."

Callie glanced at her phone. The display, her link to Ben, had gone dark.

"See those lights out there?"

Callie looked past him into the hallway. Some of the noise level had lowered, but the flashing lights were worse. They didn't seem to be coming from the office anymore.

"Those aren't Christmas lights. They're ambulances."

Callie swung back to look at his face. "What happened?"

"Attempted abduction."

"What?"

"Someone tried to grab the assistant US attorney."

The strained appearance of his face suggested more. "Ben?"

"Stabbed."

Callie shook her head in denial, but she could see from his expression it was true. "But he was just here. He went down to bring the assistant US attorney…" Her words trailed off, and she leaned back on the table to steady herself against a wave of light-headedness. "I don't understand."

"I'll explain what I can on the way."

"But—"

"Listen, Ms. Martin." He blew out a breath, softened his voice, but didn't quite manage to hide his exasperation. "We have to get you out of here. Now."

Callie was still reluctant to go with him. "Ben might need us."

"We're not doctors. The paramedics have him covered. My job is to protect you. That means getting out of here."

"Where are we going?"

He just stared at her. "How long have you been in witness protection?"

"Shouldn't you know that?"

He sighed. And glared.

"I'm sorry," she said. "I'm not trying to be trouble, but it's my life on the line here. I don't know who to trust, and I don't know you at all."

"Didn't Ben call and tell you to go with me?"

"Yes, but—"

"Ma'am, I don't want to have to drag you out of here, but the longer you stay, the more you're endangering yourself and everyone in the building."

"How?"

He stared at her as if she were wearing a dunce cap. "Despite what people think, there generally aren't random stabbings and kidnappings on New York streets."

His words cracked her bravado. Kidnapping. He was right. She needed to leave. Tears built in her eyes and emotion choked her. Bad things seemed to follow her everywhere lately.

"Okay," she conceded. Not that there was really any choice. Where else could she turn if Ben wasn't able to protect her? *Please, Lord. Guide me.*

Callie grabbed her tote bag and headed for the door. She'd learned in her first week of witness protection to keep all her essentials in one ready-to-move-at-any-moment bag. It might seem silly, but having toothpaste, a brush, her Bible and the stuffed penguin that had been a gift from her class made her feel a bit more secure in this helter-skelter world that had become her life.

"Ms. Martin." Jackson handed over her coat. Yes, she would need that. It was strange getting used to needing a heavy winter coat everywhere she went. Back home in Texas she'd rarely needed more than a sweater under her jacket when the temperatures dropped. Here in New York, they were hitting low thirties on a regular basis. Just one more thing that was different in her new world.

Callie put the bag down and slipped the coat on, taking an extra minute to zip up and wrap a scarf around her neck. She snatched her bag and started toward the door but was brought up short by the marshal's hand on her arm. Right, Ben said not to go out front.

But he was out there. Callie's loyalty to the marshal who was her only connection to her former life begged her to check on him. The tug on her arm drew her back.

"Back way," he warned. "We can't risk them realizing their mistake. Someone might still be watching the front."

Mistake? His words sank in, and Callie's knees turned to water. Her legs wobbled. The kidnappers had meant to take her? She felt suddenly as weak as if she'd been the one stabbed. Which she might have been if Ben hadn't decided to walk the attorney out first. Jackson's strong hand cupped her elbow, a support she found herself grateful for. She was still having a hard time wrapping her mind around the idea that someone wanted her dead.

Callie took a deep breath and fought for control. She could fall apart later. Right now she had to do what the marshal said. He led her toward the back corner of the offices, out the fire door and down a back stairway.

As they reached the bottom, Jackson turned to her. "There's a connecting door in the basement. We're going to walk underground until we come to the next building down. When we walk out, I want you to look calm. Pretend we're just leaving and hailing a cab."

"A cab?" That seemed so…ordinary.

"The less attention we attract, the better. There's a cab parked down the street waiting for us. As soon as I give the signal that we're coming out, he'll pick us up."

They wound their way through a warren of underground rooms, and just when Callie figured they'd walked clear to the Hudson River, Jackson took out his phone and entered a number.

"Whatever you do, don't look back. Ready?"

Callie closed her eyes and counted slowly to ten as she breathed in and out. Was she ready? No. But again, she really had no choice. She opened her eyes and nodded. "Ready."

He pressed send. They waited just inside the doorway while the clock on his phone ticked off two minutes. "Wait here until I call you."

Callie watched him stroll out onto the midtown sidewalk, the picture of New York determination as he pretended to search for a cab. There wasn't much traffic on the street—pedestrian or auto. Apparently the authorities had the entire area blocked off.

"Here he is," Jackson called. She dashed out as he hailed the cab. It pulled smoothly to the curb in front of him, but before Jackson could hand her into the car, a man in an elegant overcoat materialized in front of them, attempting to grab the ride. Callie felt Jackson go on alert.

"Sorry, sir, my wife's not feeling well. I called ahead for this car." An elbow to the man's briefcase backed up his words. Jackson shoved Callie into the cab and jumped in after her before the man could recover his balance. The driver hit the locks and the gas pedal.

Callie fell back against the cracked upholstery as the

cab sped down the block. New York traffic still scared the life out of her. She hoped she hadn't survived an abduction attempt only to be killed in a traffic accident.

Abduction. She shuddered, thinking about how close she had come to being a victim.

Callie's thoughts were interrupted by the cab pulling up to a curb. She looked around, but they didn't seem to actually be anywhere special. "Why are we stopping here?"

"Just making sure no one tailed us. We'll cross into Grand Central Terminal as if we're planning to get on a train to Westchester."

"But we're not?"

"Nope."

"Where are we going?"

"To a new safe house."

"You think this one will actually be safe?"

"Ms. Martin, WITSEC is not in the habit of losing witnesses."

"Yet you nearly did."

Callie was surprised at her bold words. She wasn't normally a complainer, but she was getting a bit tired of his terse responses and this episode had her rattled.

If she was honest, she'd been rattled for months, ever since she'd accidentally walked into the middle of a drug deal and watched her ex-boyfriend shot down in front of her.

"We have never yet lost anyone who followed the rules. And we didn't lose you."

Would it be wrong to wish they had? Callie was so tired of running. So tired of fighting for a new life. *Lord, give me strength.* She glanced over at the new marshal. *And patience.*

Four months ago, her life had been normal. Happy even. She'd been dating someone who seemed nice. She loved her job working with little children. Her church was a community that gave her support and the first sense of family she'd had in her life.

Then things started going wrong, and nothing had been right since.

She'd realized Rick wasn't the man for her. She liked him and had fun with him, but it would never grow into anything more. Though he gave lip service to her beliefs, he didn't really share them, didn't live them in his daily life. So she'd broken it off with him. Tried to break off at least. He had different ideas about that. He had different ideas about everything. That had been a big part of the problem. Things that seemed alluring at first were nothing more than temptations away from the life she'd chosen to live. So she'd ended the relationship.

And now she was paying the price for ever starting it. Facing the consequences of her bad judgment. How many times had she played the "if only" game? If only she'd stood firm. If only she'd never dated him in the first place. If only she hadn't agreed to sing backup for his band that one last time.

He'd told her it was a charity event, so she agreed to perform, even though it had been a few weeks since they'd broken up. One last time singing, and then she would put that part of her life in the past along with their relationship. Except it hadn't worked out that way. The charity gig had apparently been a cover for his drug dealing. And she'd walked right into a sting. DEA and FBI agents had arrived too late to save Rick's life but just in time to whisk her away. They'd offered her sanctuary, but in order to testify to the things she'd witnessed she'd had to give up her whole life, assume a new identity and leave behind all that she knew and loved.

As the months had gone by, she'd learned to accept this

solitary new life as atonement for her poor decisions. To-night she wasn't the only one paying the price. Regret at her own selfish thoughts stung Callie. A good man was injured, possibly dying, and another woman had been at-tacked. And what about the DEA agent?

None of this was directly her fault, but Callie couldn't shake the feeling that if she'd made better choices, it all would have worked out differently.

Jackson stepped out of the cab and surveyed the street before he reached back in to help his witness out. He of-fered his arm. "Remember, we're a couple. Look like we're out for a romantic evening."

"Is there a reason we can't just look like friends or sib-lings hanging out together?"

He dropped her arm. "Whatever you prefer."

If Ben survived, Jackson was going to have another talk with him. They'd spent an hour on the phone yesterday, going over case notes in preparation for a planned transi-tion. The trial was due to begin in two weeks, and Jack-son was set to take over and stay with Callie until it was time to bring her in to testify.

In all that conversation, never once had Ben warned him that Callie Martin was a difficult witness. In fact, if he recalled correctly, Ben's words ran something along the lines of the sweetest, most innocent Texas blonde you'll ever want to meet.

He glanced at the woman walking stiffly at his side. So much for sweet and innocent. He'd grant the beauti-ful blonde description, though. Even looking confused and scared, there was something compelling about her, something that had made him opt for pretending to be her husband rather than her brother. She'd certainly put him in his place.

"As we walk through the terminal, follow my lead. We're going to cross the main concourse, then go down the stairs to the subway."

"Why the subway?"

"I'm trying to vary our travel arrangements. I don't think anyone followed us, but if they did, it just got harder."

He guided her down the escalator along with the rest of the crowd and headed across the main waiting room. He ducked onto the Track 23 platform, then hurried her along the back corridor and out through another track door that exited through a passage, across the food market and directly into the subway. Her labored breathing caught his attention so he slowed his pace, but he never stopped moving. His gaze darted around the station, missing nothing and no one as he slid a MetroCard through the turnstile and ushered her through ahead of him.

She stopped abruptly as they approached the stairs. "Am I allowed to know where we're going yet?"

Jackson scanned the crowd swirling around them. "I'd rather not say."

He knew he was irritating her with his evasive answers. It wasn't intentional, but until he knew how her cover had been blown, he wasn't saying much of anything. For all he knew, she was the one who had arranged the ambush. Jackson glanced at her. She looked dazed and confused, not malicious. Was she innocent or just a very good actress? Either way, she was his to protect.

As they walked across the platform he thought about the expression on her face and softened. What must this look like to someone from Texas who was relatively new to New York? Santa sat behind steel drums beating out some holiday tune. Elderly ladies offered crocheted hats for sale, while a man slept crouched against a pillar. From the look of awe on Callie's face, he guessed she hadn't spent much time in the subway.

Before he could say anything, the express train pulled in. Jackson took a moment to check the platform behind them. No one seemed to be paying any attention, but better safe than sorry. He led Callie on to the train and whispered, "Stay close."

The doors started to beep their closing tune. Just as they were about to shut, he pulled her back out onto the platform. The doors popped open, then quickly closed. Jackson could hear the canned reminder not to hold the doors open. He swung Callie around and hopped on the local train pulling in across the platform.

"What… Why did we—?" Callie shook her head and grabbed for the pole as the train lurched ahead.

Jackson didn't let his guard down, but he hoped anyone who might have trailed them was as stunned by his move as she apparently was.

The local train was fairly crowded, but Jackson managed to glare his way into a seat for Callie. She sat and he stood guard over her. From that vantage point he could see everyone around. He could also see her face. She was trying not to stare, but clearly the couple across the way had caught her attention. Little wonder with their matching tattoos and red-and-green hair. He wondered how the girl from Texas was managing.

"Have you ridden the subway much?"

She shrugged. "Some. I walk when I can."

"Are you okay?"

She burst into a grin. "Yeah. I love it!"

Jackson couldn't help but grin back at her. New York might be an acquired taste, but it was good she was flexible and adjusting so well. An adventuresome spirit would make her time in witness protection a bit easier to bear.

The train pulled into the next stop, and Jackson eyed the platform. If anyone had followed them, they should still be stuck on the express. "Come on, we're getting off here."

"Already?"

Jackson bit back a smile. Was that disappointment in her voice?

He led her above ground and into the madness of the East Side at Christmas. Hailing a cab wasn't quite as easy this time, but before too long he had them back in another car. He gave directions for the West Side and watched as Callie stared out the window. "Christmas in New York. Pure insanity."

She turned to him and smiled. "I still can't get over the sheer number of people."

Something about her enthusiasm stirred a response in him. "I'm pretty used to crowds, but every once in a while it amazes me, too."

Within minutes, the cab pulled up in front of a hotel. After Jackson paid, he took her arm and helped her from the backseat. They walked to the hotel entry and waited under the awning. As soon as the cab turned the corner, Jackson urged her in the other direction.

Callie turned a skeptical gaze on him. "I can't believe anyone could still be following us—if they ever were. I'm so lost, even I couldn't find us."

"Not too much longer now."

She sighed and started walking. "You seem to know your way around. How long have you lived here?"

"I don't. I'm just here because of you. Ben probably didn't have a chance to tell you, but I was scheduled to replace him. He's needed back in Texas. I'll stay and take you in to trial."

Callie paused and rested against an office building. Eyes closed, she drew in breaths. After a minute, she started walking again. He drew alongside her and rested his hand on her arm. "What is it?"

"Nothing." She shrugged away from his hand. "I'm just still trying to wrap my head around all this. Around the idea that all of your lives are revolving around me. I feel like I should say I'm sorry."

Jackson's senses went on alert. "Why sorry?"

"That you have to be here, away from home, just because I am."

He shrugged. "It's my job." That was life as a federal marshal. Holidays were pretty much like any other day. It suited him fine.

"I don't suppose there's any chance we can stop for coffee?"

Jackson looked ahead to the familiar green sign that had caught her eye as they turned the corner. He hated the longing in her voice and that he couldn't do anything to help. "Sorry. Not until I'm sure we're clear."

She nodded and kept walking, but Jackson felt a twinge of remorse. She looked exhausted and anxious. Would it have hurt to stop? Maybe not, but he was taking no chances when they were this close to their safe house.

"This way." He glanced quickly left and right, then led her across the street and up the hotel steps. They crossed a crowded lobby, directly to the elevator bank. "We've got a room already," he said quietly. "You're going to stay here until we have a better idea what happened. There's another pair of marshals on duty up there. You'll be safe."

He hoped.

After depositing Callie in the hotel room, Jackson headed back out. He needed some information, needed to talk, hopefully to Ben if he was able, definitely to the assistant US attorney and the DEA agent. Once he'd spoken with them, he'd call his home office. They had to figure out what had gone so terribly wrong. Before it happened again.

Jackson reached for his phone to call the hospital but hesitated when he spied the coffee shop logo. The calls could wait a few minutes.

Fifteen minutes later Jackson handed off cups of coffee to the marshals on duty before entering the hotel suite.

Though Callie looked startled to see him back so soon, her apprehensive expression melted into a smile when she spotted what was in his hands. That smile made it worth all the lost time he'd spent waiting behind Christmas shoppers in a long line.

She accepted the cup from him and took a sip. "Ahh, perfect. Just the way I like it. How did you guess?"

Jackson shifted, uneasy with the praise. "It's in your file."

TWO

It's in your file.

The door closed behind Jackson, but his words lingered, sending shivers down Callie's spine. Of course she had a file. She just hadn't really thought of it in those terms before. That somewhere there was a folder—most likely on some computer database—with all her information. Even the way she took her coffee.

If her file included minor details like coffee preferences, what else did it hold? The idea that Jackson, a man she'd just met, knew her personal information, even secrets she guarded from the rest of the world, left her feeling vulnerable in a new and profound way.

Did they know who her mother was? The thought struck from out of the blue. Callie's fingers curled into fists as she fought to contain the rising dread. Wouldn't that be ironic if they knew more about her life than she did?

Callie crawled up on the sofa. Cradling the coffee cup in her hands, she gently rocked, seeking calm. How had her life come to this?

Sometimes she thought she'd been asking that same question for three straight months. How had her life gone from being ordinary—her days spent teaching kindergarten—to this constant danger? Three months ago she'd been sitting at her kitchen table writing lesson plans. Now she was in hiding from the kind of dangerous men she'd thought only existed in movies.

She couldn't even begin to comprehend all she had lost. Not long ago she'd been wondering if she and Rick had a future together. Now he was buried in his family's plot in a remote Texas graveyard, and she was left to deal with the fallout.

She didn't doubt her decision to break up with him. If nothing else, everything that followed had proved the wisdom of that choice. But with each day in witness protection, her dream of a family seemed farther and farther away.

For the umpteenth time in her life she was alone.

As a former foster kid who'd been bumped around from house to house during her childhood, she should have developed a thick enough skin to handle it. Should have. But the ache never went away. The longing for a real family remained. It especially hurt at this time of year.

Restless with the memories, Callie rose and drifted around the hotel room. It was too fancy, almost sterile. She couldn't even find a safe place to set the coffee down without fear of leaving a ring. The suite was more luxurious than any place she'd ever stayed before. New York was so far removed from her small-town Texas life.

She wandered over to the window. If Ben were here, he'd make her step back. Feeling defiant, Callie pressed her head against the glass. Fifteen floors below, people hustled along the street. For a brief time she'd been a part of that. She'd begun to settle into a new job and a new life and had actually thought it would be fun to be in New York for Christmas. She'd tried to look forward to the season, enjoying the lights, the windows, the tree at Rockefeller Center.

Now, that, too, was gone.

Heat poured from the vent, but Callie shivered as she stared at the crowds below. Evening was falling, dusk beginning to shroud the people from view. She wrapped her arms around herself, pulling her sweater tight. It wasn't exactly a hug, but it was the best she could get at the moment.

She'd allowed herself to be lulled into a false sense of security. There was no safe place for her anymore. Not only could she never go home again, but apparently she also couldn't trust that she would ever find a home that was safe. For the girl whose only dream had been a home and family of her own, that was a bitter pill to swallow.

Enough of this. Giving herself a shake, Callie turned from the window. She could wallow in sadness, or she could choose to focus on the good. And there was good. She just needed to remember it.

Callie rooted through her bag for her Bible. Focusing on reading scripture had been a tool of self-preservation in the early days of this ordeal. It was a way of reminding herself that God was good all the time. Even in the midst of all the turmoil, she had much for which to be thankful. So many people had helped her, starting with the marshals, like Ben, who were willing to sacrifice their lives to keep her safe.

Regret twisted in her belly. She wished she could have gone with Jackson to check on Ben. He'd helped her get her footing in her new life. At first he'd been a friend, protector and father figure all rolled into one. Once she'd been moved to New York, she hadn't seen him often, but he'd kept in touch. She should be there for him. Since she couldn't be, she would pray for him.

Dear Lord, I pray to You in thanksgiving for all You have given me. Jesus, my Lord, healer of the sick, please shine Your love on Ben. Protect him and keep him safe from harm.

Callie paused in her prayer. Ben had been her protector, and now Jackson had that role. She was grateful to God for sending Jackson to rescue her. Whether or not she was grateful for Jackson himself was another matter. She was going to have to get to know him better. A smile tugged at her lips as she turned back to her Bible. Buying her coffee definitely weighed in his favor.

Jackson gripped the edge of the hospital room door, trying to drain the anger from his body before facing his colleague. Ben didn't need to deal with Jackson's baggage. He had enough fighting of his own to do. According to the doctor, the knife had missed anything vital but not by much. Another quarter inch… Jackson shook off the thought. Supposedly Ben was just sleeping. Good. He'd wait.

He sank into the chair beside the bed and scrubbed his face with his hands, fighting back emotions that threatened to swamp him. Ben wasn't just his colleague. He'd been a friend, a mentor and the closest man in Jackson's life since his family was murdered.

Minutes ticked by with nothing but beeping machines and bustling nurses. Finally there was a slight movement in the bed. "You might as well spit it out instead of sitting there making angry faces."

Jackson jolted at the whispered words. Tension slid off as he looked up to see Ben staring back at him. Those sun-crinkled eyes weren't quite sparkling, but there was a light in them that eased something deep within Jackson.

He reached over and gripped Ben's hand. "Nice of you to wake up."

Ben grimaced. "You got her away?"

Jackson nodded. "Safe and secure."

Ben closed his eyes and let out a slow breath. "Thanks. I owe you."

"Nope." Jackson shook his head. Ben had it backward. Jackson owed him everything. The senior marshal had taken a wet recruit under his wing and trained him and molded him into the man Jackson was today. He didn't even want to think what would have become of the angry young man he'd been after the massacre of his family if Ben hadn't intervened. Jackson had been drifting, aimless and angry. Ben had taken the bitter youth and helped him find a purpose in life. For that alone, Jackson owed him more than he could ever repay.

For that, if nothing else, he would see that the men who'd done this paid.

"What happened?" Ben's voice melded with Jackson's.

The two men shrugged as they simultaneously asked the same important question. It would have been funny if the situation weren't so grave.

"I was hoping you could tell me," Jackson urged.

Ben frowned, trying to push past the pain. "I remember coming out of the elevator, crossing the lobby. I told Christine to let me go first, but she pushed past and went into the revolving door." Ben made a wry grimace. "She was annoyed because Callie had no answers. Said she was in a hurry. I went through the side door. That guy from DEA, Quint, followed me."

Ben shifted, focused on breathing for a minute, then continued. "Someone was waiting. I took a knife. Quint must have seen them making a grab for Christine because he shoved me aside and lunged at her. Probably saved my life, too, because the minute he got his hands on her, the car took off, and the guy who'd stabbed me disappeared into the crowd. I never even saw him."

That was not what Jackson wanted to hear. "Did you get a look at the car?"

"Quick. As I was falling. Dark blue, tinted windows." He closed his eyes for a minute, apparently drawing on his training to try to dredge up a memory. "There was a dent in the right rear bumper. Some sort of decal right above it. White and blue. I couldn't read what it said. Maybe Quint saw something else."

Jackson would check, but from the report he'd gotten earlier, Mr. DEA hadn't seen anything. He'd been totally focused on keeping hold of Christine Davis, the assistant US attorney.

"Any idea how they found her here?" Ben asked.

"Callie?" Jackson shook his head. "So you think it was her they were after?"

"Has to be. If they knew she was there, they would have expected her to be coming out with me. With Christine in that winter coat, hat covering her head, all you'd see was the blond curls. Easy to mistake."

"Still doesn't explain how they found her," Jackson muttered. "Unless someone tracked Christine or Quint."

"Possible, but we went to a lot of trouble to avoid it. That was the whole reason for bringing them here rather than taking Callie to them. Seemed safer. You came up with them, didn't you?"

Jackson nodded. "We took separate flights from San Antonio and Austin into Atlanta but got stuck on the same connecting flight because of weather delays. Never acknowledged each other in the terminal or in the air and we made sure to take cabs to different hotels. No one would have had any reason to suspect we were together unless they knew."

Their gazes met and held, neither wanting to be the one

to say the words, admit that one of their own must have leaked information.

Ben finally broke the silence. "Get her out of town." He swallowed hard, as much from the pain of betrayal as from physical injury. "Don't tell anyone. Just go."

"There's one other possibility," Jackson offered.

Ben shook his head slowly. "Nope. Makes no sense."

Jackson didn't respond.

"It's not what you're thinking."

"How do you know what I'm thinking?" Jackson demanded.

Ben rolled his eyes. "Because I know you. She's not in cahoots with them."

"You still want to say that? You're lying in this hospital bed because someone stuck a knife in you."

"They were trying to get to her."

"So you say. How do we know they weren't trying to help her escape?"

Ben gave him a look of disgust.

"Why wasn't she with you anyway? Why did you have Christine instead of Callie?"

Ben closed his eyes briefly. "Christine had come down really hard on her. Basically accused her of withholding evidence. Made all sorts of threats. She had Quint there giving his best DEA glare, trying to intimidate her."

"Did it work?"

"Depends on your point of view. Poor kid was shaking in her boots. But she didn't have any information to give."

Jackson leaned back in the chair and studied Ben's expression. Had his mentor gone soft?

Ben shrugged self-consciously. "I wanted to give her some time to settle down. It's been real hard on her. So I left her in the office and took Christine and Quint down. I figured I'd ask them to lay off terrorizing the witness—at least until the holidays were past, you know?"

Jackson nodded. He knew. That was just the kind of thing Ben did. Going above and beyond to be sure his witness was not only safe physically but emotionally, too.

Jackson was careful with his words. "That doesn't mean she wasn't involved."

"Gut instinct says she's innocent."

Jackson snorted. "Is that your healthy gut speaking or the one that was knifed?"

Ben laughed weakly. "Good one." He closed his eyes.

"You're tired and I've got to get back to my witness." Jackson stood and rested his hand lightly on Ben's shoulder. "Take care. Don't worry—I'll keep her safe until you come back."

When Jackson turned to leave, Ben grabbed his sleeve. "Seriously, man." He paused, dragged in a breath. "Don't go into this thinking she's guilty. If you do, you might make a mistake that costs her life."

Jackson looked down at his friend. He couldn't say the words, but he nodded his promise.

As he made his way back to the hotel, Jackson replayed the scene in his head. Ben was right, of course. He had to keep an open mind. Honestly, it didn't matter at all to WITSEC if she was innocent or guilty. She was a protected witness who could provide testimony to convict the real bad guys. For that reason alone, she had to be kept safe.

It was a job he took very seriously.

THREE

By the time he reached the hotel, Jackson was envisioning dinner. He could have stopped to pick up something for them, but he decided to indulge his witness and let her choose. Maybe that would put them on a better footing.

The lobby was mobbed with Christmas revelers, so Jackson ducked around back to the lesser-used elevator bank. He squeezed in with a couple of bellhops and a room-service cart. The news was playing on the elevator television screen, and Jackson immediately recognized the scene from this afternoon.

He could just barely make out the news anchor's voice over the chatter. "In other news, the Christmas season took a dangerous turn this afternoon when armed robbers tried to mug a woman exiting an office building in midtown. The woman escaped unharmed but her companion is hospitalized with a knife wound. Police are asking anyone with information about a late-model, dark blue SUV to contact the number showing on the screen."

So that was the story they were giving out. Innocent mugging. Jackson shrugged. It wasn't like they could reveal the truth that the assistant United States attorney responsible for prosecuting the biggest drug cartel of the past decade had almost been abducted on a Manhattan street. Not good PR for New York or the Texas justice system.

Jackson was turning his focus back to dinner plans when another conversation caught his attention.

"Dude, look." One waiter nudged the other and pointed at the screen.

Jackson glanced up in time to see a quick flash of Christine Davis's face on the screen. Uh-oh—someone would not be happy that picture had been released.

"The blonde? Nice."

"No, man. The car. See the car? That looks like the one I saw parked right outside on 55th when I went for my smoke break."

"I thought you stopped smoking."

"Forget that. The car I saw. It looks like the one they showed in the picture. Even had the same dent."

Jackson froze. Ben said the car had a dent. He looked up, but the news had moved on to another story.

"You think there's a reward?"

The first guy hesitated. "A reward is nice, but not if it costs me this job."

"I thought you were on break. It's not like you were sneaking out or something. Talk to the boss."

"Yeah. Let me just deliver this burger to 1408 first."

Jackson fiddled with his phone, pretending to read a message, then reached over and pressed a different button to get off at the floor below Callie's.

He took off down the corridor, through the fire exit and up the flight of stairs, taking the steps two at a time. He dashed down the hall and flashed his badge at the man standing guard. "Inside. We've got trouble."

The marshal took one look at Jackson's face and started defending himself. "No one saw her, sir."

"What?"

"The room service. I placed the order and I accepted the food. She stayed in the bedroom. No one saw her."

"That's not the problem, and it's not your fault." Jackson wanted to kick something. The only person at fault was him for leaving her. How had they managed to find her again already?

He burst into the room, calling to Callie to grab everything. "We're leaving."

"Again?" She sighed. "Can't we wait until I finish eating?"

"No. Staying to finish could cost your life."

"Don't you think that's a little extreme?"

"I just rode up in the elevator with hotel staff who recognized the car that was used this afternoon. It's parked outside the hotel."

She looked confused. Little wonder.

"Which means that somehow they know that you're in the hotel."

Jackson began searching the hotel room for anything to use as a disguise. When he returned to the main room, Callie was still standing there looking dumbstruck and on the verge of tears.

"Look, Ms. Martin. You can think about this all you want later. Right now, we need to disguise you and get you out of this building before they figure out where in the hotel you are."

He asked the other marshal for his coat and hat and shoved it at her. "Here, take this. Turn it inside out and stuff your hair up into the hat. Where's your scarf? Wrap it around your face."

He watched impatiently as Callie did as he'd directed. "Make sure there's no hair showing and let's go. We can't disguise anything else now. We have to get moving."

He turned to the marshal. "Once we're clear, say five minutes, call it in. If anyone else shows up or asks about her, tell them—" He looked down at the tray. "Tell them she went out to dinner."

Jackson opened the door and scanned the hallway. "Come on."

He took her by the hand and led her down the hall away from the elevator. "We're taking the stairs."

"Fifteen flights?"

He stopped long enough to recognize the panic settling over her. "No," he reassured. "Down four and then I'll wait for an empty elevator."

Once they reached the eleventh floor, Jackson kept her hiding in the hallway until an empty elevator arrived. He pulled her into the corner, shielding her from view as other guests got on. When they reached the fifth floor, they got off and he led her through a maze of conference rooms and down a series of escalators until they came out in a back alleyway onto 54th Street. He was tempted to swing around the block and take a look at the car, but it wasn't worth risking his witness. A sudden peal of sirens in the distance told him the call had been placed. Now to make good their escape.

A line of cabs was waiting, but Jackson didn't want to leave a trail from the hotel. Grabbing Callie's hand, he dashed through traffic, crossed the street and ducked into the lobby of another hotel. He turned to face her. Callie was gasping for breath.

"It's okay. We'll get a cab from here to the airport."

She looked upset, on the edge of breaking down. Once he had them settled in a cab, he wrapped an arm around her and rested her head on his shoulder. "Hang on," he whispered. "We're almost clear."

By the time they arrived at JFK, Callie had recovered her color and some spunk. Jackson led her into the terminal, where they ducked into a shop to buy some tourist gear and cheap reading glasses. He sent her into the bathroom to fix up while he called to arrange a rental car.

His phone rang just as the car arrived. A quick glance at the display revealed his boss on the line.

"Walker here." He juggled the phone while he traded car keys for a tip. He considered moving to another space, but Callie should be out soon. He'd use his badge if necessary to keep the space.

"I hear you stopped by to see Ben." John Logan's voice held more understanding than censure.

"Sir. I don't like operating blind. Just wanted some answers."

"Which is why I'm calling. Figured you couldn't come in for an update."

"I'm better off on the move."

"Agreed. The car was abandoned."

Jackson listened as his boss filled him in on the details, then blew out a breath of frustration. "Any sign of them?"

"Nothing."

Jackson didn't like the sound of that. Were they still searching the hotel for Callie? He didn't think they could have been followed, but it wasn't likely the thugs had just given up.

Jackson stared into the distance, watching the planes take off and land. There was a pattern to it, a rhythm. Most things had one. Few occurrences were random, including today's attack. "What are you thinking?"

"Someone found her and wanted to send a message. Take her or take her out."

Jackson chewed on that for a minute. He didn't like the taste. "You don't think she's involved?"

"Callie Martin?" His boss sounded surprised. "Nope. I don't think so. You do?"

Jackson was relieved his concern wasn't dismissed out of hand. "I haven't talked with her long enough to form an opinion. It just seems likely."

There was a long pause. "You aren't the first to question it, but most change their mind after getting to know her a little better."

Jackson acknowledged his superior's unspoken advice to give her time. He still intended to stay alert—and not just when looking for the bad guys.

"Let me know when you're settled in. I'll see to backup."

"Will do, thanks."

As Jackson disconnected the call he turned and found Callie standing behind him. How much had she heard? Enough to be suspicious—and angry—based on her expression. She walked silently to the car, climbed into the backseat and settled against the door, all without looking at him.

Jackson put away his phone and climbed into the front. He turned the key in the ignition, put the car in gear and headed west.

Miles rolled away under the wheels of the rental car while Jackson mulled over his conversation with Ben at the hospital. Something was nagging at him, but he couldn't figure out what exactly it was.

He glanced at his witness in the backseat. She made him uneasy, too. He'd protect her, but he wouldn't be fooled. You didn't last long in witness protection if you let the witness burn you.

As the hours passed, the hum of the tires on the blacktop began to lull Jackson. Fatigue burned his eyes and the lane lines started to blur. He needed sleep. Coffee would have to do. The last sign had indicated a rest stop in twenty miles. He had to be pretty close to that now.

Traffic had been light and there was no indication anyone was trailing behind them. He'd varied speed enough and watched the cars carefully as they passed, so he was 100 percent confident no one had followed him. Still, when he saw the exit, Jackson skipped using the turn signal and waited until the very last second to make an abrupt turn into the rest-stop parking lot. There was no sense in advertising his plans. He pulled in close to the rest station and turned to check on Callie. The slow rise and fall of her chest and her gentle, even breathing told him she was deeply asleep, as she had been ever since they'd left the airport. He probably should wake her and see if she needed to go inside.

"Ms. Martin?"

She muttered something in her sleep and huddled deeper into the seat.

He didn't like leaving her alone, but he'd do neither of them any good if he fell asleep at the wheel. Hopefully, he'd be back and on the road without her ever noticing he'd been gone.

After a quick stop in the restroom, Jackson stocked up on coffee and candy bars. He was just exiting the building, ripping open a candy bag with his teeth, when a bloodcurdling scream echoed across the parking lot.

Callie! Jackson dropped the coffee. Candy pieces scattered in his wake as he ran for the car.

"Ms. Martin, Callie, Callie, wake up."

The words came from a great distance. Callie felt the hand on her arm and screamed again. "Let go of me!"

"Callie." The voice was gentler now, closer. "Callie, you're dreaming. Wake up."

She could barely hear his words over the thrum of her racing heart, but the soothing tone helped ease her terror. It was a dream. He said she was only dreaming. Oh, praise the Lord—it was all a dream.

As her fear ebbed, Callie's memories rushed in. Screams rose in her throat again, but she cut them off with a sob.

"That must have been some dream."

She buried her face in her hands, rubbing her eyes as if she could erase what she saw. It wasn't a dream, not really. It was her living nightmare. She'd been reliving the night Rick was killed.

"Are you okay?"

She lifted her head and looked around, noticing for the first time that they were in a parking lot. The back door of the car was open, and Jackson was crouched beside her.

She nodded in answer to his question and raised one of her own. "Where are we?"

"Somewhere in the middle of Ohio."

Which meant they'd driven through New Jersey and Pennsylvania while she'd been sleeping. "Is that where we were going?"

He shrugged. "I was just driving until the sun came up."

It dawned on her that he'd been driving all night while she slept. "Do you want me to drive for a while so you can sleep?"

There was only the barest hesitation, but she caught it.

"No, thanks. I thought we could find a hotel, pull in and catch a nap for a while."

The last thing she wanted to do was sleep again.

He returned to the driver's seat, and she took the passenger side. They sat for a while, each lost in their own thoughts, until Jackson broke the silence.

"Do you want to talk about it, the dream?"

"Not really."

"It might help to talk. Get it out of your system." He winced. "Sorry, not a good choice of words."

"I understand." And she did. She just wasn't anxious to relive the experience a second time tonight. "Maybe some other time."

"Do you have these dreams often?"

"No." She paused. "I haven't had one in weeks. Not since I settled in New York. I felt safe there, I guess." She could hear the defeat in her own voice. Safety was an illusion. "We should probably get going again, right?"

He didn't answer. She could tell he wasn't going to let it drop, but she couldn't deal with any more of it tonight. She had to change the subject.

"I fell asleep before I could ask you about Ben."

"That's okay—you were exhausted." And angry.

"How is he?"

"Fortunate to be alive. The knife missed anything vital. He's just weak from blood loss."

"Thank you, Lord." Callie fiddled with the latch on her seat belt. "Did he explain what happened?" And would Jackson tell her if he had? Callie hadn't forgotten the snippet of conversation she'd overheard. Did he really think she was involved in yesterday's attack?

"Just that as he walked out of the building with the assistant US attorney and the DEA agent, one person knifed him while another tried to snatch Christine. Quint managed to hold on to her."

"But someone identified the car?"

"Apparently there was a security camera on the building. They got a still from that. It matched the car they found outside the hotel, but no one was inside."

Callie collapsed back into the seat. "If they attempted to grab the attorney, why does everyone think they're after me?"

The silence stretched so long Callie began to fear Jackson wouldn't answer. She watched his fingers on the wheel, reading the tension in his grip. Finally he eased up. "Ben thinks they mistook her for you, you both being tall and blonde."

Callie wanted to be offended that the woman who'd

been so harsh could be mistaken for her, but she could see Ben's point. They had similarities, especially in heavy winter clothing. With a sinking heart, she mouthed the words she feared. "Do they want me dead or alive?"

She watched Jackson take a deep breath, then let it out slowly. He glanced over at her before answering. "I can't honestly say." He took his hand from the wheel and reached over to cover hers. "But I can promise I'll do everything in my power to keep them from getting to you."

She swallowed around the sudden lump in her throat. "Thank you."

The silence was broken only by the hum of the tires on the highway. Callie chewed on her lip. "So we assume they're still after me."

"Apparently so."

She sagged against the seat, trying to absorb the implications. "Then what do we do now?"

He jerked his head toward the road. "For the time being, we keep driving."

"Doesn't really sound like much of a solution," she muttered.

"Ms. Martin—"

"Call me Callie, please. With all the time we're spending together, Ms. Martin seems too weird. That's what my students call me."

He chuckled. "Wouldn't want to be mistaken for a five-year-old."

Callie didn't even crack a smile. "Why would they go to all this trouble if not to kill me?"

Jackson shrugged again. "They could have been trying to send you a message. Let you know they could find you."

Callie shuddered. "They sure made their point."

Jackson turned the car on and pulled back onto the highway. "Ms. Martin, Callie, it really would help me to protect you if you could tell me about your dream, tell me what happened."

"I thought it was all in my file."

"The facts are there. I need to understand you, know how you feel."

"What, to see if I was involved?" Callie tossed that out just to see how he reacted. It seemed everyone's first impression was to think she was a part of this.

"You seem pretty calm about such an accusation."

Callie bit her lip to fight back tears. "I've had lots of practice." She swallowed hard. "It's everyone's first reaction. Apparently no one can believe that someone could be completely in the dark about what her boyfriend was up to."

"But you were."

"I was."

"Tell me."

So finally, she did. Maybe because she desperately wanted him to believe her, she told him each harrowing detail. About how she'd been lonely so she kept dating Rick long after she'd known better. How she'd gone along to gigs with his band, helping out as a backup singer whenever needed. How despite everything, they'd drifted apart because they wanted different things from life. How she'd finally broken up with him—even before she learned about his lies and deceptions.

And then there was that final night. Rick had begged her to sing with them. Said he needed her, and the kids who would benefit from the fund-raiser needed her. She'd always been a soft touch for a child in need and he'd known it.

She recalled how they'd performed a first set, and then the guys had taken a break to go outside for some air.

Callie stopped there. She buried her head in her hands

and prayed for the strength to get through this retelling, for the wisdom to find the words that Jackson needed to hear, for the courage to continue her fight for justice.

"I was chatting with one of the families from my school. They'd come into the cantina for dinner. The family had twin girls who'd been in my class several years ago. I sat with them, catching up about everything the girls were doing.

"After a while, it hit me that the guys had been gone a really long time. It was getting awkward to still sit there because the family was ready to leave. So I decided to go find Rick."

A sob escaped her lips as she got to the next part. "I stopped in the ladies' room first." She looked up at him through tear-drenched eyes. "Do you know how many times I've wondered what would have happened if I hadn't stopped in there first?"

Jackson reached back across the seat and squeezed her hand. Callie realized he had pulled off the road again and was sitting, facing her, giving her his undivided attention.

"I was almost to the patio door when the first shot sounded. I didn't realize what it was at first, fireworks or something. I wasn't expecting gunfire. But when I pulled back the door, I was suddenly face-to-face with a man holding a gun. He turned and waved it at me, then blasted it off at Rick." She twisted the scarf in her hands, wringing it, wrapping it around her hand, over and over. "He fell at my feet."

Such simple words. *He fell at my feet.* They didn't begin to capture how it felt to watch the life flow out of him, to watch as the recognition in his eyes faded away into a blank stare. Chaos had erupted around her, with federal agents bursting in and capturing the gunmen. That was all a hazy memory. She'd had eyes only for Rick. She'd stood there like petrified wood as his blood pooled around the pointy toes of her favorite boots.

Callie ripped the scarf off her hands and yanked the car door open. She had to get out, get away from the memory. She paced along the deserted highway, only vaguely aware of Jackson trailing behind her.

"Callie."

She turned around. His arms were open, and she fell into them. He wrapped his coat around her and held her close while she cried.

When the sobs finally lessened, she lifted her head. "That's why I didn't want to tell you the story tonight. This happens every time. They keep telling me it will get better with time, but it never does."

FOUR

Jackson awoke to a sound at the door.

He bolted from the bed and grabbed his gun. The sound came again, a soft knock, and he relaxed, realizing it was coming from the connecting door.

After he'd gotten Callie back in the car early this morning, they'd driven another hour before stopping for food and then finally settling into adjoining hotel rooms.

He'd lain awake long hours, replaying the scene she'd described, trying to see through the emotion to the truth. Had it happened as she said, or was she a stellar actress?

The taste of doubt was bitter on his tongue, but Jackson knew the price of false belief was much worse. He wanted to believe her, but if he was going to keep her safe, he had to be completely sure he understood every angle, every dynamic.

He'd finally dozed into a fitful sleep, but based on the slant of sunlight coming through the window, it hadn't been for very long. He shrugged into his shirt before opening the door.

"What's up, Callie?"

"Hope I didn't wake you."

Her distrust from yesterday appeared to have given way to a reluctant acceptance and friendliness. He supposed he could go along with that. If they were going to spend a week in close quarters, they might as well be friendly.

He yawned. "I wasn't really sleeping well anyway."

"Yeah, that was quite the bedtime story I told you."

Jackson laughed, but the look they shared said they both knew it had kept him awake. "Let's not talk about that now." He could offer her that much anyway. "I'll grab a shower and then we can go get some lunch, okay?"

"Can we walk through the Christmas Fair?"

"The what?"

"While you were sleeping, I read the local paper. Today is their Christmas Fair. It started with a parade earlier this morning, but there are activities all day—caroling, ornament making." Her head dipped in resignation. "I know we can't really do any of those things. I'm sorry. I shouldn't even be thinking about it after what happened yesterday."

She was right. They'd come a long distance with no sign of a tail, but that didn't make it playtime.

"I feel like I've been either sleeping or running for the past twenty-four hours. The past three months really. It would be so nice to do something normal."

The shadows under her eyes reminded him of how hard this had been on her. Not as hard as being dead, though.

They'd run in so many circles and switched transportation so many times, it should have been impossible for anyone to have followed them. Jackson wasn't taking any chances on should haves. Still, her sad eyes tugged at him.

He was known for being overly cautious, but maybe there was no real cause for concern since they'd gotten cleanly away.

"Let me check in with the office. If there's no indication anyone followed us, then we'll see. We have to eat."

"Really?" Callie beamed at him and something inside

him lifted. "I know you don't like it, but…I just really need something normal today, you know?"

He didn't know. Not really. There wasn't much about his life that was normal—ever—but he did understand her need. Her life had just been turned on its head a second time. Normalcy was necessary, even if it was an illusion.

Jackson grabbed some fresh clothes and headed into the shower. He needed some time alone to rebuild the professional wall he'd breached when he'd held her in his arms last night. The embrace had been natural, an offer of solace to a fellow human in need. He hadn't expected to be the one feeling comforted.

An hour later, with the car packed and ready to move at a moment's notice, Jackson drove them into town. It was his concession to her desire to walk. He'd drive to town, then they could walk and catch a bite to eat. His office said there was no indication of trouble, no evidence they'd been trailed. He guessed they could handle an hour in one small town at Christmas.

There was a huge lunch smorgasbord at the Church Hall and Callie talked him into eating there. Up until yesterday she'd roamed freely around New York City, she reminded him. As Jackson watched her chat with the locals and drink in the festive atmosphere, he decided the change was good for her. She had a knack for making friends and fitting herself in, which would suit her well in witness protection. Whereas he would have stayed back, grabbed a burger at the corner diner and been on his way, she'd jumped right into the thick of the celebration. After the harrowing past twenty-four hours, it was nice to see her relax.

An hour became two, and Jackson was more than ready to move on. "Callie."

She grinned at him, and it was such a contrast to her frightened, shell-shocked expression of yesterday that he found himself grinning back. But they were still leaving.

As they walked out to the car, she touched his arm to stop him. "Can you give me just five more minutes? There's something I need to buy. The pastor's wife told me I can get it in that little shop on the corner."

"Callie, we really need to get moving."

Her face fell. Jackson kicked himself. Maybe it was female things she needed.

"Five minutes."

She ran off, promising to be back in four.

Jackson leaned back against the car and stared at the small shop she'd entered. No female things in there. What could she possibly need from a trinket shop like that?

Whatever it was, she was true to her word. He'd watched the numbers on his phone advance only three minutes when she came dancing out the door.

Jackson grinned looking at her. Ben was right. She was charming when she was happy. He watched her come down the steps of the gift shop, her cheeks rosy from the cold, her lips curved in a smile that hinted of happy secrets.

She started to cross. Instinct had him on alert, so he sensed the car almost before he saw it. He yelled a warning as a dark vehicle came barreling around the corner. Too late he realized it was coming directly between him and Callie. The wheels screeched as the driver skidded to a halt and two men jumped out.

Jackson charged across the street, yelling for help. He pulled his gun and tried to take aim, but he couldn't get a clear shot. There were too many families to risk shooting. He ran faster, but it felt like concrete blocks were dragging at his feet. Everything moved in slow motion as one man grabbed Callie around the waist and the other one shoved her toward the open car door.

There was no way he could reach her in time.

Callie heard Jackson's yell a split second before a black SUV cut to the curb in front of her. Tinted windows made it impossible to see inside. She had no time to react as men jumped from the car and grabbed her.

No! She hadn't gotten this far just to let them take her now. At least not willingly. She screamed and kicked as hard as she could.

She may as well have been kicking cement for all the good it did. One man had his hands around her wrists like manacles while the other held everyone off with his gun.

Callie stopped struggling. There were too many children on the street. She couldn't risk one of them being hurt. She heard Jackson yelling as they shoved her into the SUV. The door slammed behind her, the engine raced and the car leaped forward.

Facedown on the seat, Callie couldn't see anything, but she felt the car gathering speed. Her heart sank. It was over. Despite all the precautions. She should have listened to Jackson, should have stayed in the hotel room. Now, because she'd wanted to celebrate Christmas, there would be no one to testify against the killers, no one to see justice done for Rick.

No. She wasn't giving up. As long as she was breathing, there was still a chance. Rick may have made poor choices, but he hadn't deserved to die for them and she wasn't going to make it easy for his killers to dispose of her. Hopefully there would be time for regrets later, time to tell Jackson she'd do whatever he asked. First she had to figure a way out of here.

Callie held herself very still, not an easy feat as the car

careened down the road. She tried to get her bearings, evaluate the predicament. There were three men—the driver, the one she thought of as the gunman and the one who had grabbed her. None of them was saying a word, but the tension in the car was intense. Was someone—possibly Jackson—following them?

The gunman fired a shot out the window, and Callie's heart seized. *Please, Lord, don't let him hurt Jackson. None of this is his fault.*

"Can you see who's following us?"

Based on the direction of the sound, Callie attributed the question to the driver. She couldn't make out the reply. Without moving her head, Callie eased an eye open. She couldn't see anyone so she waited. When there was no reaction, she slowly turned, moving her head in minute increments until she could see ahead. Unbelievably, no one seemed to be paying attention to her. Maybe they thought she'd been stunned when they threw her in the car. The driver was concentrating on the road and the gunman held his head just inside the open window, his gun outside and aimed at the car in pursuit. The man who had grabbed her, and who was probably supposed to be watching her, had turned his back to play lookout. "Speed it up. He's gaining on us."

Sirens crowded the air and filled Callie's heart with relief. The feeling lasted only an instant; it was replaced by fear as the driver hit the gas harder and the lookout pulled out his weapon and began firing. She was going to have to do something to improve her odds if she wanted to survive.

Callie took a minute to consider the possibilities. It would have helped to know the rules. Was she supposed to be taken alive, or didn't it matter if they only delivered her body? Knowing that answer would improve her chances of making the right choice of who in the SUV to attack.

Because she didn't know, she'd go with the one thing that was clear in her mind. Being taken—dead or alive—was not an option she was willing to consider.

The driver seemed the best choice. She had little chance against a man with a gun, but if she could take the driver by surprise maybe she could crash the car.

"How are we doing?" The driver barked the question at the man in the passenger seat.

Good. She'd like to know that, too.

"They're falling back." He took aim and let off another shot. "Got a tire. Another few shots, and we should be clear."

Which meant she had no time to lose. The next time he took aim, Callie did, too. She launched herself between the seats and wrapped her hands around the driver's face.

"Hey, someone get hold of her." The driver shook his head violently, trying to free his face, but Callie hung on for dear life. Blinded by her hands, he lost control and the car careened off the road.

Callie felt the barrel of a gun connect with her jaw just as the car slid off the pavement.

Crash. The impact rolled her onto the floor. Stunned by the double assault, she lay there a minute. Pushing past the pain, she scrambled to her knees just as the door flew open. She could have cried at the sight of Jackson's face. Never had there been such a sweet image. He pulled her free as police officers surrounded the car.

Jackson grabbed her, half carrying, half pulling her across the street to the safety of his car. Once she was safely inside, he rounded the car, got in and locked the doors. "Get down until we know the area is secured."

His voice was harsh, just like it had been the first time she'd met him, and Callie had a flash of insight. This was his tense voice. The one that said the situation was not to his liking and needed to be controlled. Given his ability to control, that tone was reassuring to her. While sheriff's deputies swarmed the SUV, Callie ducked down beneath the seat as instructed.

Within only a few minutes, Jackson gave the all clear and helped her up because the officers had all three men out and spread-eagled against the car. Callie could only stare in disbelief. It had all happened so fast. Less than twenty minutes ago she'd been shopping. It was terrifying to think how quickly things could change.

"I'd prefer to hit the road and get out of here," Jackson said. "But I think we'd better stay and answer some questions. We don't want the sheriff tailing us, too."

Callie nodded. Her heart was still racing too fast for her to form an answer.

"Just stay here while I—"

Callie reached and grabbed his arm. Panic was beginning to settle over her now that the immediate danger was past. "Please, don't leave me."

Jackson's gaze softened. "Don't worry. I'm not going anyplace. I'm just going to stand outside the car so the officer can find me." He got out and rooted around in the trunk before unlocking her door. "Here, have some water and try to relax."

He crouched beside her seat. "You're safe now." He waited until she looked at him, until she let his assurances wash over her.

"Okay." She nodded. "I'll work on believing that."

He winked at her. "That's my Callie girl."

She gave him a feeble smile, then winced as pain rocketed through her jaw. He tilted her chin and stroked a finger over the sore spot.

"We've got to get some ice for that bruise. Do you want a paramedic?"

"No. I'll be fine."

Jackson stood, closed and locked the door with his key fob, and leaned against the car, waiting for the sheriff's deputy to come speak to him.

Inside the car, Callie forced herself to take deep, calming breaths, but this time her heart was racing as much from his endearment as from her near kidnapping. *His Callie girl.* No one had ever called her anything like that before.

It didn't mean anything. He was just caught up in the moment of worrying about her and feeling protective. That was okay. It still felt nice to have someone care for her.

Once Callie calmed down, it didn't take long for her to grow restless. She started to get out of the car, but seeing Jackson in the middle of a serious-looking conversation with the local police officer, she decided to wait. What were they saying? Didn't they need to talk to her? She'd been the victim, after all.

But what should she say? What was Jackson saying? This was witness protection—not an ordinary crime. How much would a marshal give away in a situation like this? She'd have to remember to ask Jackson so she didn't make any mistakes about it next time.

Next time. The thought hit Callie squarely in the chest.

She started to tremble as she acknowledged the simple truth. There was always going to be a next time. Despite Jackson's reassurances, she wasn't safe and she never would be again.

How many times did she have to be reminded?

Her breath came short and fast as waves of heat rolled over her. The air in the car was suddenly stifling. She lifted her hair and rolled it into a bun, trying to keep the damp mass off her neck. She tried to roll the window down, but the power switch didn't work with the car off so she rested her cheek against the window, hoping the chilled glass would cool her. *Please hurry, Jackson.*

She closed her eyes a moment and concentrated on breathing slowly, in and out, in and out. She opened her eyes to check on Jackson just in time to come face-to-face with one of her kidnappers as he was dragged off by the police. Their gazes met for just one second—one interminable second of staring into the face of someone who wanted her dead. The look in his eyes was lethal. Heat switched to chills. Goose bumps rose along every inch of skin as Callie shivered uncontrollably. She let her hair back down and wrapped it like a shawl, huddling into the door, trying to curl in on herself as despair swamped her.

Lord, help me. Help me to find Your purpose in all of this. I am Your servant, Lord. I am Your servant. Callie whispered the prayers as she choked on silent sobs. Why was this happening? There had to be a bigger purpose. That was the only way any of this ordeal made sense. At least that's what she kept telling herself. But what was that purpose? What was she supposed to do?

Is this Your plan for me, Lord? What do You want of me? I am Your servant, Lord. Maybe if she repeated them enough, the words would break through the despondency that cloaked her.

Jackson was still conferring with police officers, so Callie continued to pray. Gradually the words calmed her fears, and her agitation eased. God didn't want her to be passive. She might not understand exactly what His purpose for her was, but she was pretty sure it didn't involve being anybody's victim. She continued the prayers, calmer now. *Show me what to do, Lord. Lead me.*

By the time Jackson got back in the car, she was settled and resolute. "What did they say? What's next?"

"They took the men in on attempted kidnapping. The

sheriff asked us to stop by the station to file a report. No need to go any further than that. There were enough witnesses. We can leave your sworn testimony and contact info. And get you some ice."

"I can leave contact info?" She massaged her jaw as she waited for him to explain. "How does that work if I'm in witness protection?"

Jackson shrugged and waved it off. "Don't worry. I'll give my cell number and leave a number for the marshal's service. If they have to call, we'll get the message."

Callie interlaced her fingers, running one thumb over the other as she struggled for composure. This was just one more reminder of how different her future would be. Even giving contact information required advance planning.

They drove in silence for a few minutes. As the car pulled up in front of the station, Callie turned to face Jackson. "I don't know how to ask this exactly, but what am I supposed to tell them?"

"What do you mean?"

"I'm not supposed to tell anyone my real name, but I won't lie."

"You won't lie?" He looked so puzzled by her refusal. Callie watched him mull over her words. She could almost see him rolling them around inside his brain. Finally he nodded. "No problem. It's fine."

"How so? I'm not kidding. This is important to me. I always tell the truth."

"It's not a problem, Callie. We gave you a new identity, so you might as well give them your real name."

"Okay." Her tension eased. "Thank you."

He nodded. "And just so you know, Callie. You're not lying when you tell people your new name. Legally it is your real name."

She wasn't ready to think about that.

"Okay." She couldn't think of anything else to question, so there was no postponing it. She was going to have to face the men who had just tried to kidnap her. The men who were somehow connected to the ones who had killed Rick. She closed her eyes a moment and drew on her strength. *I can do all things in God who loves me.* She opened her eyes and turned to Jackson. "Come on. Let's do this."

FIVE

Two hours later, when they left the station, Jackson could see that Callie was exhausted. Despite her brave front, she had to be reeling from the nonstop action of the past few days. Having to face a lineup of men who had just tried to kidnap her would be trying for most people, but Callie had managed it seemingly unfazed. Her poise and determination amazed him, but they were clearly taking a toll.

Jackson's every instinct shouted that they should push on, get as far away as possible, but maybe it made more sense to stay here overnight. Callie wasn't the only exhausted one. He was still tired from the previous sleepless night, and although he was trained to do without sleep, there was no sense taking unnecessary risks.

If he could be sure there was no one else around beside the men who'd been arrested, maybe he'd take the chance, but he didn't want to get caught alone on a highway with no one around to help.

Staying where they'd already been found made no sense either. He needed to check in with his boss and see if they could figure out what was going on. The local sheriff could hold the men for kidnapping, but Jackson wanted someone from either the FBI or DEA up here to interrogate the trio of kidnappers.

The local sheriff would make sure charges were filed appropriately, but he didn't know the background and Jackson couldn't tell him. The sheriff was no dunce, though. He knew there was more to the story. An attempted abduction of a woman traveling under the protection of a federal marshal likely set off all sorts of alarms. Protocol prevented Jackson from telling him the full story, but the man had clearly read between the lines. He'd looked Jackson straight in the eye and said, "If I ask why this woman is with you, you're going to tell me she's your cousin or sister's friend, so I won't waste your time asking. Just tell me what I need to know and anything you need from me to keep her safe."

Jackson appreciated that support more than he could acknowledge. Until he could get backup he trusted, he and Callie were in a vulnerable position. He didn't like it, but he had to trust this sheriff, so when the man had recommended a place to stay for the night, Jackson had accepted.

"Callie?"

She startled, and Jackson realized she'd been asleep. "Sorry. I didn't realize you were napping."

Callie rubbed her eyes. "Not really. Just dozing off and on. Cars make me sleepy."

"I know we ate earlier, but I figured with all the excitement, you might be hungry."

She yawned, confirming his decision to stay for the night. "I could eat. I guess. Is there anyplace around here open this late?"

She had a point. Christmas lights still twinkled in store windows, but the shops themselves were dark and everyone seemed to have gone home.

"Sheriff told me there's a twenty-four-hour truck stop that has decent food. It's right off the interstate."

"That's nice." She yawned again. "Honestly, a soft pillow sounds more appealing."

He smiled at her. "That can be arranged, too."

"You seem quite adept at arranging things."

"Not so good at keeping the bad guys away, though." That irked him. He'd been so careful, changed cars, watched for a tail. He'd seen nothing and no one who gave him any sense of being followed. He didn't like this feeling of failure, the sense that he'd missed something.

The alternatives weren't good either. Jackson didn't really want to consider that someone was leaking information on their whereabouts, but it was looking more obvious. He glanced over at Callie huddled into the corner of the car. She seemed legitimately scared, rattled by her experience. But was it all an act? Had she actually led the men to her?

Had he foiled an escape attempt rather than a kidnapping?

Jackson let the question roll around in his brain a bit. He mentally weighed the pros and cons. The cons were winning. It didn't ring true to think she was involved. If her version was true, she'd facilitated her own escape. Something had caused the driver to lose control. There was no reason to believe it hadn't gone down as she'd said.

And there was her whole refusal to lie thing. She'd seemed sincere.

But someone had given them away.

Unless she was carrying some kind of tracking device.

"Callie, did Ben ever sweep your stuff to make sure there was no GPS tracking device on you or any belongings you have?"

"Yes. He checked my belongings and gave me a new phone just to be safe."

"Good." But somehow they were still being tracked,

They needed to get settled for the night so he could make some phone calls. He wanted to change cars again, too.

At some point he was also going to have to deal with the fact that he'd almost lost his witness tonight. She could easily have been shot because he'd let her go into a store unprotected. Guilt gnawed at him, but his professional side shoved it deep so he could concentrate on protecting her now. Later he'd deal with the guilt. Now he had to concentrate on making sure it didn't happen again.

Callie's squeal of delight interrupted Jackson's troubled thoughts. He'd pulled up in front of a Victorian house that looked like it belonged at the North Pole. Seemed the sheriff had a sense of humor.

"Is this where we're staying?"

Jackson peered through the darkness for the house number. Santa was holding a sign that said "Welcome."

"I think so. The sheriff said his sister gets a bit carried away for the holidays. But her house will be a safe place to stay."

"I think it's great."

The energy level in her voice lifted Jackson's spirits. Callie had a great ability to rebound. Not to mention a crazy love of the holidays.

Half an hour later, when they were ensconced in a Victorian parlor sipping peppermint-flavored hot chocolate, he was the one yawning while Callie chatted animatedly with their hostess. Yes, she would do fine in WITSEC if he ever got her safely into hiding. She had a genuine affection for people and an ability to find something in common with most everyone they met.

"How did you and the chief hit it off so well?"

"Hmm?" Jackson looked around and realized he and Callie were alone again. He must have drifted off while she'd been sharing Christmas decorating tips.

"This." She spread her arms wide. "It's a far cry from last night's accommodations. Not that I'm complaining. I was just wondering how you rated so with the chief that he sent us to his sister."

"We both served in the army in Afghanistan."

"You knew him?"

"No." How could he explain they'd just recognized something in each other? He shrugged. "It just came up."

"A bond you share?"

That was pretty perceptive. "I guess you could call it that." That bond was the main reason he'd been willing to accept the offer of overnight accommodation. Without exchanging a word directly on the subject, the sheriff had let Jackson know he understood the situation and would see to their safety. No one but the sheriff and his deputies would know where they were staying tonight and they'd be on the road before dawn. It wasn't his favorite scenario, but it was the best option available The sheriff wouldn't have willingly put his sister at risk, so that made Jackson feel a bit better.

"I didn't know you served. Thank you."

Jackson smiled at Callie. She was a constant source of surprise. "You're welcome. But I should be thanking you." At the quizzical tilt of her head, Jackson continued. "You've been extraordinary. So brave and resilient. I know this hasn't been easy on you."

She shrugged. "It's not like I really have any choice."

And that said more about her than she realized.

"There's something I meant to ask earlier. Why did you go into the store? Did you buy anything that could have attracted attention?"

"I don't think so. I was just buying you a present."

Jackson blinked. "You've known me only slightly more than twenty-four hours. Why would you buy me a present?"

Callie smiled sweetly and suddenly Jackson had to fight to hear her response over the rush of blood in his ears. "It's Christmas. And you're risking your life to keep me safe. It's not anything big." She got up and rummaged through her carryall. "Here." She held out a Christmas gift sack.

Jackson reluctantly accepted the bag. He peered inside it and found an insulated travel mug.

Callie smiled with a grin as wide as any kid's on Christmas morning. "I figured if we have to keep running, at least you can have hot coffee."

"That's sweet. Thank you." Jackson was genuinely touched. Later he'd let himself dwell on his suspicions and wonder if she had been trying to throw him off or find a way to be by herself so the guys could grab her. But for now, he'd accept the gift at face value and be grateful.

"We are staying here, right? For at least tonight?" Callie drained her cup and looked at him expectantly. Jackson could see she was fading fast. Her eyelids were drooping, and she'd stifled more than one yawn in the past few minutes. He covered one of his own.

"What a tired pair we are."

She tried to laugh, but it faded into yet another yawn.

"Go on off to bed. I'll see you in the morning."

Callie grabbed her bag and headed for the stairs. She stopped in the doorway and turned back to him. "Thank you for everything, Jackson. You've been pretty extraordinary yourself." She gave him a little half smile that he knew would be lingering in his mind long into the night.

"Try to sleep," she admonished. "The deputies will be watching, right?"

He nodded, not trusting his voice.

"Good night."

She was right. He needed rest, but he doubted he'd sleep anytime soon. This paradox of a woman had his mind racing. Could she possibly be as innocent and sweet as she seemed?

And while he was puzzling that through, maybe he'd find the answers to some of the other questions that were plaguing him. Like why the men had attempted to kidnap Callie. If they wanted her dead, it would have been easy enough to take her out. Even on the crowded street, they could have gotten off a clear shot. That was going to haunt him for sure, but a more immediate question diverted his attention from that blame game. Why had they tried to kidnap her instead?

Something was off, something he couldn't quite place. Maybe his boss would have some answers.

When that call went straight to voice mail, Jackson decided it was a sign to at least try to get some sleep. Grabbing his bag, he headed up the stairs and down the long hallway to the room his hostess had shown him earlier. He stopped beside Callie's door and listened. The sounds were soft and muffled but unmistakable. She was crying. The sound struck right to his heart and left him feeling helpless. He could protect her, but he couldn't change what her life had become.

The ringing phone jolted Jackson from a fitful sleep. It took a moment for him to register the unfamiliar number as the local sheriff's office.

"Walker here."

He listened calmly at first, but disbelief soon transformed into fury. "Let me get this right. You knew several hours ago that the men who attempted to abduct Ms. Martin escaped—okay, were broken out." He paused, fighting back the words he wanted to say. "And you're just calling me now because…?"

He had to repeat what the deputy said because it defied

imagination that they had waited so long. "Because you found the car they used to escape." Jackson clenched and unclenched his left fist. "And no one considered that Ms. Martin might be in danger because the men who tried to take her earlier were back on—"

Jackson broke off as his own words registered. Beads of sweat popped out on his forehead. "I'll call you back." He raced down the hall and pounded on Callie's door. "Callie, Callie. Are you in there? Ms. Martin. Open the door or I'm coming in."

"Hang on a moment."

The sleepy voice was the sweetest music to his ears.

Callie, hugging a huge plush robe around herself and rubbing her eyes, opened the door. "What's wrong, Jackson? It's not morning, is it?"

She looked so adorably sleepy that he wanted to hug her. And that meant he needed to smack himself a reminder. What was he even thinking? This was about protecting her life, not noticing how attractive she was.

Where had that idea even come from?

"Callie, please step out into the hall. I need to search the room." He tried to sound businesslike but not alarming.

Apparently he'd failed. She was wide-awake now and grabbing his arm. "What happened now? What's going on?"

Jackson paused. He hated that the words he needed to say would worry her. She'd been through so much. He noted her puffy eyes. Remembering the sound of her tears, he hazarded a guess she'd cried herself to sleep. Now he was about to sink her right back into her misery.

"Jackson?"

"I just got a call from the deputy." He saw her face fall, knew that he didn't even need to finish the sentence, but he did anyway. "They escaped."

There was a moment of pure panic on Callie's face as

she looked around. "You think they came here? Is that why you want to search my room? I don't want to stay out here alone. Let me stand in the room with you while you search. You don't really think they're in there, do you? How would they know where we are?"

Her panic broke his heart. Life was so unfair sometimes. Here she was just trying to do what was right and she couldn't even get an uninterrupted night's sleep.

His phone rang. Jackson glanced down and realized it was the sheriff's number again. In his concern for Callie, he'd forgotten to call back. Hopefully they had good news.

"Yeah?"

It wasn't the news he wanted. "Okay. Yeah, I understand. Send someone over to lead me there."

He disconnected the call and turned back to Callie. One look at her face told him she wasn't planning on staying behind.

"Apparently someone tampered with food that was delivered to the sheriff's office. While the deputies were passed out, someone broke in and let the prisoners free. They ditched the escape car just outside of town. The sheriff asked if I want to come down and take a look."

"I'm coming with you."

Jackson knew Callie would need more sleep, but he had no intention of letting her out of his sight. "I wish I could leave you here, Callie. We've got long days ahead and—"

"You think I can sleep knowing the men who tried to kidnap me just broke out of prison? You think they won't be coming for me?"

He didn't have an answer for that. Not one he wanted to give her.

"Besides," she continued. "I was the one they took. Maybe I'll see something you miss."

Jackson refrained from commenting on his years of

training and experience, partly because the desperation in her eyes stirred something in him, but also because his gut instinct said to bring her along. Separating just felt like the wrong thing to do.

"Let me check out the room before you go change. Then I'll tell the sheriff you're coming."

Callie flung her arms around his neck. "Thank you," she whispered. "I promise not to get in the way."

She was as good as her word. When they reached the scene, she stayed back with the local officers while Jackson investigated. There was nothing there to tell him much more than they already knew. Discarded food wrappers indicated four people had been traveling, which meshed with one person breaking out the other three.

But where were they now? And what were they planning?

Another deputy got off his phone and walked over to the sheriff. A few minutes later, the sheriff signaled Jackson to join him. "Car was stolen one town over. Report just came in."

Jackson kicked the tire. He hadn't really been counting on getting anything from a rental agency, but there'd at least been a chance. They had less than nothing now.

"So the fingerprints probably belong to the owner."

"Probably."

"Did anything show up from the fingerprints you took at the station?"

The sheriff shook his head. "Not in the system."

Jackson grunted his frustration. "Any chance of tracking anything away from here?"

"There were some footprints in the mud, but they only went as far as the highway. They must have had another car waiting."

Which meant there might be five or more men after Callie.

None of this made sense. Why send five men after a witness when one sniper would do? Did they want her dead? Or just want her?

SIX

Callie shivered in the cold night air. She stood at the edge of the road, pacing between the sheriff's car and the police tape. The deputy she'd been entrusted to had suggested she stay in the car, but Callie needed to be moving, needed to be able to see Jackson.

Her heart was racing and she felt light-headed, but still she paced. The tingling in her toes and fingers could have been from the cold, but it wasn't. This chilled, out-of-control feeling had nothing to do with the temperature and everything to do with her feelings of helplessness. She didn't like this new version of herself, this woman constantly on the verge of a panic attack, so dependent on her marshal to keep her safe.

Jackson would tell her to cut herself some slack. It wasn't every day a gal survived two attempted kidnappings within forty-eight hours. Knowing that didn't change how she felt, though. It didn't regulate the chills or alleviate the impending sense of doom.

Only prayer could do that.

Lord, it's me, Callie, again. You're probably sick of hearing from me by now. Please help me get through this. Please show me Your will. She looked over to Jackson, who was conferring with the police chief. *Thank You for sending Jackson to me. Please protect him, watch over him and guide him.*

She was still praying and pacing when Jackson came up behind her. He rested an arm around her shoulders and drew her into the safety of his arms. "How are you holding up?"

She felt stronger in his arms. Not invincible, but better. She tried to smile reassuringly, but the minute her gaze met his, tears welled up. The understanding and compassion in his eyes washed over her. "Okay. I'm okay."

He gave her shoulders a squeeze before letting go. "We can leave now. There's nothing more here."

"Did you learn anything?"

He shrugged. "Some. I'll tell you in the car. Sheriff's going to lead us back into town. He'll have another car follow. Just to be safe."

They climbed into their car, but he didn't speak. He just reached across and took her hand. How had he known she needed that? Needed the simple human contact to reassure her that she wasn't alone in this.

It was a mistake to rely on him for anything more than her physical safety. He was her marshal, her protector. Nothing more. He could never be anything more. No matter how much she was growing to like him.

That didn't mean she couldn't cherish this one small moment of peace—the comfort that spread from his hand to hers. They rode in silence, a caravan of official vehicles following the winding back roads into town. Jackson kept their hands linked, allowing the deep quiet to envelop them in a temporary haven.

As the car pulled up in front of the office, she turned to him. "Thank you. I needed that."

He didn't ask why. Didn't question her. He just nodded

as if he understood, and his sad smile told her that maybe he had needed it, too.

But the time for peace was past. She needed to know what was going on. She withdrew her hand and focused her attention. "I can handle it now. What did you find?"

Jackson turned away and sat with his hands resting on the steering wheel, his neck and back held erect. She could see him draw in a deep breath and slowly exhale before he answered. His eyes stared straight ahead.

"There are at least four of them."

Callie gasped. She hadn't been expecting that. "Four?"

"Or possibly more. The three who were in jail and the one who broke them out. Someone else was driving the new car. We don't know if that was the same one who broke them out or another. Then there was whoever got to the food delivery. Sheriff has a deputy out checking that angle. They're not making much progress. I'm hoping our office can do better."

Four, five, what did it matter how many there were? The idea that they were after her, that anyone was so determined to get to her, still amazed Callie. And reinforced her determination.

"If they sent five people after me, then it must be really important that we elude them and I stay alive to testify." She took a moment to bow her head in prayer, to ask for grace. "Tell me what we need to do. I'll do exactly as you ask."

She knew she was putting a huge burden on him, but together, and with God's grace, they could prevail.

He nodded slowly. "Okay. But in the morning. Neither of us has had much sleep in the last two days. We'll need sleep to be alert. Let's try to catch a few hours while the local guys keep watch. We'll plan fresh in the morning. Okay?"

She smiled at him. "Sounds like the best plan I've heard yet, but…"

Callie hesitated. "What?"

She shrugged. "I'm not questioning your judgment, but they did let the men escape. Are you sure we can trust them to keep watch?"

Jackson leaned toward the steering wheel and rubbed his eyes. When he lifted his head and turned to answer, she could momentarily see all the responsibility of his job weighing on him. "I'll be honest. I don't love it. But it's the best we can do right now." He smothered a yawn. "The sheriff invited us to stay at his own house instead. He'll have extra men on."

"Does he know the truth, what's really going on?"

"No." Jackson shook his head. "But he's no fool, and he figured out it's something important. These men are very determined."

"And on that note, let's have sweet dreams." Callie laughed nervously.

Jackson took her hand again. "If it would make you feel safer, we can drive on. I'd just feel better doing it in daylight. Don't want the boys catching up to us alone in the dark."

Callie gave him her best brave smile. "I trust you."

She did. She'd known him less than two days, but she'd trust him with her life. Which was a good thing since that's exactly what she was doing.

He had to check in with his office, so it was close to three by the time Jackson found his way to bed. He was anxious to get back on the road, but what he'd told Callie was true. They were both too exhausted to leave now. He really needed another marshal or two, but even if he was willing to risk the leak and ask for help, it would be a day or so before anyone could catch up with them, especially because he had to keep changing direction. Once he figured out their next step, he'd reconsider having someone meet them. In the meantime, he had to trust that with the guard of squad cars and sheriff's deputies, they'd make it safely through the night.

Trust. Not a word he was comfortable with. Jackson was much better relying on himself, but in order to be any good to Callie tomorrow, he had to trust in the locals tonight.

That was easier said than done for a man who was used to being the one in control. What his brain told him was best and what his instincts demanded were in direct conflict. An hour later, he was still tossing, and sleep was merely a precious dream. His body cried out from fatigue, but his mind kept racing in a semiconscious mode halfway between sleep and wakefulness, working through all of the puzzle pieces that didn't quite fit together. How did today's abduction attempt fit in with the office attack? Had they correctly interpreted the threat to Callie? What if they didn't intend to kill her?

That was the question that kept him awake. Why would someone try to take her alive? A message? A threat? Or something else? Those endlessly circling questions had him up and pacing the room as an uneasy feeling settled in his stomach.

Had that foiled kidnapping attempt really been meant for Callie, or had they been trying to send a bigger message by getting at the attorney who would be prosecuting the trial? He knew she was under guard now, too. Did she connect back to Callie in any other way? Had they known each other before? And the underlying thread that gave all these questions a bad smell—how had his witness's location been discovered?

Jackson collapsed against the wall and slowly sank to

the floor. He sat hunched over, head resting on his knees as he buried his face in his hands. He couldn't begin to contemplate the idea that any of the men he'd looked up to for so long could be anything other than model marshals. He had no reason to think otherwise.

Just a nagging feeling of doubt. A doubt that had never been there before. He'd only ever held his fellow marshals in the highest esteem.

And he would continue to do so until there was proof to the contrary. Jackson scrubbed his hands over his face, trying to rid himself of the disturbing suspicions. It was probably only the lack of sleep addling his thinking. They had likely all been victims of someone who had infiltrated the office.

Someone was going to a lot of trouble to get to Callie. The question was, why? She either had to have something they wanted or she knew too much.

If Callie knowing too much was the explanation, why didn't they just shoot her when they had the chance? The fact that they hadn't raised some serious questions. How much did she know? More to the point, why did she know it? Because she was an unfortunate witness? Or because she was a part of it?

Jackson considered the frightened woman who'd clung to him earlier. Her fear was tangible, and it came across as genuine. Of course she could be in cahoots with them and still be afraid. He rubbed his eyes, pinching his brows together as he tried to make sense of the whole ugly picture.

He mentally replayed the interactions he'd had with Callie since they'd met. She'd been stubborn, even made a few foolish mistakes, but nothing all that different from mistakes other witnesses had made. There was something different about her, but he didn't think it was guilt. It felt more like naive hope or a belief that things would still work out. It was hard to believe it was all an act on her part.

But that put him no closer to understanding what it was all about and no closer to falling asleep. He finally gave up and headed down to the kitchen to brew a pot of coffee. He was on his third cup, head buried in a newspaper, when Callie arrived for breakfast.

The aches and pains from his sleepless night were a welcome tradeoff for the bright smile on her face as she entered the breakfast room. At least one of them had caught some sleep.

"Good morning, Jackson." Her cheery greeting and happy smile were more potent than the coffee in his mug. She was so resilient. Where did she get it from, that ability to bounce back no matter what?

She poured some coffee and grabbed a doughnut from the box the sheriff had left on the counter. "Are we the only ones here?"

Jackson sipped his coffee, trying to find the energy to match her mood. "Sheriff's still asleep. He didn't get in until just an hour or so ago. He said to help ourselves to anything in the fridge."

Callie smiled that sunny smile at him. "Good. I love to cook. Let me see what I can find. Don't you just love big, old-fashioned kitchens like this? The kitchen is my favorite room in the house. There's something so cozy and inviting about being in a warm kitchen with all the good aromas from cooking food."

Yeah, cozy. That's just how he was feeling. Jackson took a slug of coffee. He was glad she was in good spirits, but her enthusiasm was making him realize just how tired he was.

Callie set about scrambling eggs. "You need more than coffee."

She was right, but the idea of eating didn't settle well in his stomach right now. "I already ate, thanks."

She gave him a dubious look but proceeded to make her breakfast. "So, I have an idea."

Those words said in that chirpy voice did not bode well. "Really?"

"I think we should set up a trap."

"Excuse me?"

"These guys keep coming after me. So, instead of waiting for them to strike again, we should set up a trap for them."

There wasn't enough coffee left in the pot. That was Jackson's first thought, his defense against an idea he could never allow.

"Callie, I appreciate that—"

"You didn't let me finish. We'll set out as if we were leaving and drive somewhere obvious so they'll find us. When they do, we'll call for police backup and head off to some lonely spot where we'll wait for the police to show up and—"

"The sheriff will never agree to that."

"But…" Callie clearly wasn't giving up. "That way we'd be in control."

Jackson sighed heavily. "One of the first things you learn in this line of work, Callie, is that you're never sure how things are going to work out, so you just don't take those kinds of unnecessary risks. Certainly not with a civilian."

Callie did not look happy to be thwarted. "I'm not just any civilian. I'm their target. They've gone after me twice in as many days. What makes you think today will be any different?"

When Jackson didn't answer, she pushed her plate away, folded her arms and leaned back in the chair. "Do you have a better plan?"

SEVEN

Apparently Jackson's plan was to just hit the road, but he hadn't taken into account the craziness that was holiday traffic on the last shopping weekend before Christmas.

Callie hummed Christmas songs to herself as they crawled along the highway. She'd grant him that stopping off at the sheriff's office and sneaking out the back to pick up a waiting new car was clever. But that had been an hour ago, and they'd barely gone twenty miles.

"How can there be so much traffic in such a small town?"

Jackson practically snarled in response, and Callie burst out laughing.

"Oh, come on. You've got to admit it's funny. You didn't want to follow my plan, and here we are like sitting ducks in a Christmas parade."

Jackson muttered something under his breath that Callie suspected she was better off not hearing.

"At least you have hot coffee."

He made a face. "Do you have any idea how much coffee I've consumed today?"

Callie couldn't help herself. She started humming the Grinch song. Jackson looked over as if to check he was really hearing what he thought he was hearing. She just smiled innocently. He chuckled and returned his attention to the traffic ahead. It was finally starting to clear.

Callie knew she shouldn't give him such grief. The poor man looked like he'd barely slept a wink in days. By contrast, she was in a ridiculously good mood this morning, probably a reaction directly proportionate to the attacks on her life. She was so happy to be alive that nothing as silly as a traffic jam was going to destroy her mood.

"How do you do it?"

Callie looked up. "Do what?"

"How do you stay so upbeat in the midst of all this?" He waved his hand at the line of stalled traffic, but she sensed he meant the whole situation they were in.

"By 'this' you mean that someone has tried to kidnap me twice and that we have men after us who broke out of jail and somehow they keep finding us?"

"All that and you're singing Christmas songs."

"I like Christmas." Callie knew she sounded defensive, but what did the man want—for her to curl up in a ball and cry all day? She'd done enough of that in the month after Rick's death. It hadn't accomplished anything, and it certainly hadn't made her feel better.

"I like Christmas, too, but when men try to abduct my witness in broad daylight on a small-town street, I guess it kind of spoils the mood."

Callie agreed. "Well, yes. That was a little sobering."

"Sobering?" His chuckle was more like a full laugh now. "I think it's a little more than that."

"Okay, I'll grant you that, but what choice do I have? I *am* going to testify against them. If they're clever and determined, then we have to be doubly so. But that doesn't mean I have to be in a foul mood."

"Was that a dig at me?"

Callie looked up, startled. "Not at all. I doubt you got much sleep, and all the pressure of keeping me alive is on you. You're entitled to be a little grouchy."

"Uh, thanks."

Callie shrugged dramatically. "Drink your coffee. Do you want a doughnut?" She offered one from the box the sheriff had given them.

"I want a cookie."

"If you give a mouse a cookie," she teased.

"Huh?"

"Just a little kindergarten teacher humor. That's the title of one of the books my kids loved."

"So tell me about Callie the kindergarten teacher."

Callie was surprised by the request. "Why?"

"We're stuck in a car together, and we can't talk about the bad guys all day. Tell me about cute kids. Maybe it will make me less…grouchy." He glanced over at her and winked.

Callie felt that wink to the tips of her toes. Oh, he was a charming one.

"What do you want to know?"

"Why did you become a teacher?"

She didn't answer right away. Jackson looked over and lifted his shoulders in question. "Was that a difficult question?"

Callie stared out the side window of the car, blinking at the bleak landscape. Funny how minutes earlier the cold air and bare trees had made her anticipate the holidays. Now they just depressed her. "Do you want the quick answer or the real one?"

"Both. Quick one first."

"I love kids, and teaching gives me the opportunity to spend my day building hope into their lives, helping them see what they can become."

"Sounds impressive. Now what's the real answer?"

Callie leaned her head against the glass and closed her eyes, thinking back into her past. It was a lonely place she didn't like to visit even in her memories. But something about Jackson made her feel safe, as if it was a good thing to share.

"I was a typical foster kid, bounced around because no one could keep me. The only stability I had was school, and there wasn't even always that. But I had this one teacher." Callie had to stop and blink back the tears. She swallowed hard. "Second grade. She made me believe it could get better. She gave me hope."

"Sounds like a special lady."

Jackson's words wrapped around her like a warm blanket. "She was. I hoped she would adopt me since she didn't have any kids of her own."

"She didn't?"

"No."

"Callie?"

"She was killed in a car crash. Apparently she'd had a fight with her husband and took off. The roads were icy. We don't do ice very well in Texas. Her car slid off the road."

"I'm so sorry."

"Thanks." She cleared her throat. "There was no one who would take me to her funeral, so years later, I went to visit her grave on my own. I vowed that I would try to give other kids the same hope she'd given me. And now I can't.

"If you want to really understand me, really know why I'm determined to bring these men to justice, then know it's because they took that away from me. I can't work with my class anymore. I can't even teach other children because I'd be a danger to them. They killed Rick, and they took away the only thing I wanted in my life—to make a difference to children who need someone."

She was quiet for a bit, struggling for calm. "I'm sorry. I know that was way more intense than you anticipated."

"You're wrong."

Callie swiped at the tears rolling down her cheeks. That was not the response she'd expected. "Wrong about what?"

He reached across the seat and took her hand. "I'm sorry they took that from you. But just from knowing you a few days, I know you'll figure out a new way. It might not be what you planned, but you've got more grit, more courage than most people. You'll figure out a way to do this."

She smiled at him through her tears. "Thanks for the pep talk. Do they teach that at Marshal School?"

"Smart aleck. But I'm glad to see you smiling again. I'd even prefer you singing Christmas tunes to crying." He patted her hand playfully as she reached to turn on some music "I'm serious, Callie. We'll make sure you get to testify, and then we'll find a place where you can make your difference. That's a promise."

"Don't promise, Jackson. I don't like promises."

"Are you going to explain that?"

"No. I think I've done enough of the pitiful act for one day. Let's talk about you instead. How do you celebrate Christmas?"

"I don't."

She waited but he didn't add anything. He suddenly seemed very tense. His hands were clenched tightly on the wheel, his arms so rigid they'd snap if anything touched them. What could possibly be so awful in his life that he'd reacted so strongly to her simple question?

"Don't look now, but I think we have company."

Callie turned around to look over the seat. Sure enough, a dark gray SUV was traveling directly behind them, keeping back far enough so as not to be suspicious, but that only made it more suspicious.

"Get down, Callie. I don't know what they're planning, but there's no sense making a target out of yourself."

Gone was the gentle man of a few minutes ago. In his

place was the tough marshal she'd first encountered back in New York. His voice demanded immediate compliance. She didn't want to get down and not be able to see what was going on, but common sense said she needed to do what Jackson told her.

"Do you want me on the floor or just slouched down?"

"For now keep your seat belt on and slouch down below window height. Be ready to move instantly onto the floor if I say so." He glanced into the rearview mirror and changed lanes.

Callie couldn't see anything ahead of or behind her, but she felt the car speed up. From Jackson's angry mutterings, she suspected the car behind had done the same.

"Here." He tossed his phone to her. "The sheriff's private number should be in recent calls. Call him. When he answers, give me the phone."

Callie did as directed, waiting through interminable rings before the call was answered. "Hi, Sheriff. Callie here. We're in a bit of a jam, and Jackson needs to talk to you."

Callie handed over the phone, then listened as Jackson apprised the sheriff of their situation and location. It took all she had not to peek over her seat to see what was happening. Jackson's ever-increasing speed gave her enough sense that it wasn't good.

The sound of something hitting their car wasn't good either.

"Jackson?"

"Callie, I need you to crouch down in front of the seat— wedge yourself in as tightly as you can and hold on to whatever you can find. It's going to get bumpy, but you'll be out of the line of fire down there."

Resisting the urge to look out the rear window, Callie unclasped the seat belt and slid to the floor. She curled herself into a ball. Jackson shrugged out of his jacket and tossed it down to her. "Pull this over you and try to use it to cushion your head."

"What's happening?" The tremors in her voice probably gave away her fear, but Callie was beyond caring.

"Someone fired at us." He sounded like he was speaking between clenched teeth, so Callie decided it was better not to distract him. She turned her attention to God instead. "Lord, help us," she whispered. "Surely You didn't bring us this far to die in a car crash."

The car suddenly swerved. Callie bit her lip. She didn't want to bother Jackson but she needed to know how desperate the situation was. As if in answer to her unspoken question, she heard Jackson say to the sheriff, "I need both hands. I'm going to hand the phone off to Callie. She can tell me what you're saying. Here, Cal, take this."

Callie reached for the phone and then tucked herself back into the small space. "Hi again."

"Hey, Callie. Hang in there, kiddo. We'll have you out of this in no time."

"Good to know." She hoped he wasn't just trying to make her feel better.

"Sheriff wants to know why you don't just put him on speaker?"

Jackson had taken his eye off the road only long enough to hand Callie the phone, but already he could see the momentary distraction had given his opponents an edge. They were closing in. "Tell him we're bouncing around too much. It'd be too difficult."

"Okay." She relayed the message and listened. "He says there's a turnoff up ahead. You won't see it until you're on it so let them think they're getting close, then swerve off road at the last minute."

"If it's so hard to see, how will I not miss it?

"You heard that, did you, Sheriff?"

Callie chuckled. It was an absurd sound, given their tense situation, but it helped settle him.

"He says there should be a big red barn coming up on the left side. On the right there's a sign for a Christmas-tree farm."

"I see them."

"Right after the tree-farm sign, make a hard right. It won't even look like a road at first, but there's pavement under there."

"Barn's coming up on the left." Jackson eased up on the gas enough to slow his speed without giving away his intention to the pursuers. They were speeding up as if the game was just about up. Good.

"Tree farm sign coming up in ten, nine, eight, seven. Hang on tight, Cal—this is going to be rough." Jackson gripped the wheel as tightly as he could and braced himself against the seat. At the very last moment, as the car in pursuit closed in, he swerved sharply to the right and accelerated, hoping that the chief was right about there being a road under all the overgrowth.

The other car surged forward past them, and Jackson breathed a sigh of momentary relief. It wouldn't be long before they'd turn around and be after him again. The other car was a bigger SUV and would be able to handle being off road better. Jackson made a mental note to choose something like that when they switched this car out. Provided they lived that long.

Anger flared at the thought. He was responsible for Callie's safety, and somehow he'd failed yet again to protect her. Had he put her in danger, or was there something else going on here? If he was going to keep her alive, he needed to get to the bottom of it and fast. But right now he needed to concentrate on getting them safely out of this situation.

"Sheriff says this is an old logging road. Keep straight."

A squeal of tires behind him alerted Jackson that the chase was on again. They wouldn't be fooled as easily this time. "Tell him they're on my tail again. How long?"

Callie repeated the question and waited for an answer. "They're setting up a roadblock on the other side of the hill."

"What hill?" Jackson shouted. The land all around him was hilly. Frustration gnawed at him, and his temper grew shorter with every foot the enemy gained.

"Do you see a sign up ahead for a swimming hole?"

"No."

Jackson could hear the sheriff's impatient reaction through the phone. Yeah, he understood all about that.

"He wants to know how far back they are."

Jackson darted a look in the rearview mirror. He'd come around a curve about half a mile back. They hadn't cleared that yet. "Half a mile, a little more."

Callie relayed the information. Later, when they made it through this, he'd tell her just how impressed he was with her clearheadedness under pressure. She was acting more like a partner than a client.

"I think he is, but I'll ask." She turned to Jackson. "He wants to know if you're a good driver."

Jackson did not like the sound of that. "Yeah."

"Willing to do something risky?"

Right now he was willing to do whatever it took to get them out of this.

"Just tell me what to do."

"Can you describe for him where we are now?"

"On a road surrounded by trees. I know, not very helpful. We just passed another sign for the Christmas-tree farm. One mile ahead."

"Good. That's what he's looking for. The road is pretty straight for three-quarters of a mile, then it makes a sudden left curve before the entrance to the farm."

"Okay."

"He says go as fast as you feel safe. Slow as you come to the curve, then accelerate into it and follow the curve around but be ready to steer out of it and into a hard right into the entrance to the farm." She paused and listened again. "You can speed down that lane. It's well maintained and fairly flat."

Jackson laid his foot on the pedal and felt the car leap forward. "Won't they figure that's what I've done?"

Callie relayed the question.

"He says probably, but that's okay."

Jackson could hear Callie moving around on the floor. She had to be getting pretty cramped. "You're doing great, Cal. Just ask him why it's okay."

Callie waved her finger outside of the jacket, signaling him to hold on. "He put me on hold a minute," she whispered. "No, I'm still here. Oh, that's great. Okay. Where are we now, Jackson?"

"About to take the turn into camp."

"Any sign of the car behind us?"

Jackson glanced in his side mirror. "Nope."

Callie relayed his answers and after a minute spoke to him again. "He says go about two miles down the road. You'll pass a house on the right and a parking lot on the left. You should see the truck they use for hauling trees in the lot."

"Okay."

"You're going to love this, Jackson. The guy who owns this farm is a friend of the sheriff. As soon as we get past, he's going to pull that tree truck into the driveway as if he's headed into town. We'll have clear sailing out the back way and the deputies will be waiting back on the road for the bad guys.

"And the sheriff says not to worry—he'll have road-blocks set up in case they miss the turnoff to the farm. They can't get out any other way."

"Great. Tell him I owe him."

There was a pause while she repeated his thanks.

"He says it's his honor to help. So can I come out now?"

"Give it a minute. These guys took shots at us, remember? I wouldn't put it past them to try again if they're desperate enough."

"Okay."

Jackson smiled at the mix of resignation and triumph in her voice. He felt pretty much the same as he sped down the road past the farmhouse. He waved a salute to the man in the tree truck and reluctantly kept on down the road. He'd love to stop and see them caught, but it would be foolish to waste the precious time. No repeating last night's mistake and hanging around. Someone else could follow up. He was getting his witness safely out while he could."

Five minutes later he heard the muffled ring of his phone and Callie's voice answering it. "That's great! Thanks, Sheriff."

She emerged from the jacket and crawled back onto the seat. "They've got them all in handcuffs."

Jackson steered to the side of the road and rested his head against the steering wheel as he drew in steadying breaths. She was safe. "Good job, Cal."

"We make a good team, don't we?" She was beaming at him in a way that made him feel like he'd just conquered Everest.

"You know what the best part is, Jackson?"

EIGHT

I dare you to not like Christmas after that.

Hours later, Jackson couldn't stop her words from re-playing in his mind. He kept thinking that for a woman who liked Christmas so much, Callie was having a pretty bleak season. On the run, far away from everyone and ev-erything she knew. Separated from the class she loved so much. Pretty dismal makings for a holiday.

Maybe he could do something about it.

First, he needed some information, even if it meant put-ting himself out there.

"You awake over there?" He knew she was awake, but she'd been sitting huddled in the corner for too long.

Callie stretched and opened her eyes. "Yeah."

"You okay?"

"Yeah."

"Cat got your tongue?"

"I haven't heard anyone use that phrase in…well, in like, forever."

"I haven't heard you have so little to say…in…like, days."

Callie laughed. "Feeling playful, are you?"

"Hey, we survived what looked like a pretty desperate situation. I think we have a right to feel anything we like." He left the words dangling.

"What?" He was finding it really hard to resist that grin. "What was the best part, Callie?"

"Christmas trees saved us. How many people do you think can say they were saved by Christmas trees? I dare you to not like Christmas after that."

Callie matched his silence for a time. Finally she surrendered. "Is that your way of asking how I'm feeling?"

Jackson sighed dramatically. "I never was very good at subtlety." He concentrated on the road ahead for a few miles before speaking again, hoping she'd say something. "I'm worried about you, Callie. This has been a pretty stressful few days."

She flipped her hair back and tugged the scarf tighter. "The things they don't warn you about in witness-protection bargaining."

Jackson didn't have an answer for that. Witness protection was a serious business, a dangerous one. "How are you handling it?"

"I'm dealing."

"By talking to yourself?"

"What?"

"You were talking to yourself back there. I heard the murmurs."

Callie stared at him like he had grown an extra head. "I wasn't talking to myself, Jackson. I was talking to God."

"Huh?"

"I was praying, talking to God. Asking Him for help."

Jackson didn't have a response for that either. He couldn't remember the last time he'd prayed. At least not seriously. Probably before his parents had been killed. It certainly hadn't been since. "It helps you?"

"I couldn't have made it through any of this without knowing God was watching over me." She smiled. "So, yeah, I guess it helps."

He nodded. It was obvious she wanted to press him, but his lack of a prayer life wasn't really the point here.

"So is religion why you love Christmas so much?"

Callie chewed on her lip for a moment before answering. "Yes and no."

"Explain."

"Well God sending his son to redeem us is the only reason the season exists, and church on Christmas is such a blessing." She broke off and fiddled with her scarf again. "But if I'm being honest, it's the whole family thing, the tree, the food, the hours spent with friends and family, the lights, the decorations. All of that shouts Christmas to me." She paused and her voice dropped a notch. "I guess we idealize what we don't have."

"But you had some good experiences?" He was pushing, but he didn't like the funk she seemed to have fallen into. He needed to break her out of it.

"Yes. The teacher I told you about. And there was this one older woman. I really wanted her to be my mother, too."

Jackson could hear the longing still in her voice. "Why couldn't she be?"

"She was too old and sick, though I didn't realize it at the time. She couldn't physically handle raising a young girl."

"I'm sorry." The words seemed inadequate.

"Thanks. She was pretty special. She didn't have much, but she lived her life with such joy. She taught me that happiness can be found in little things, in the simple acts of sharing time together.

"We were in Texas so we never had snow for Christmas, but one year she took some of us in for the holidays so we wouldn't have to stay alone. She filled her house with scented candles so it would smell and feel like Christmas even if it didn't look like it.

"She was the one who introduced me to Jesus. She gave me a children's Bible for Christmas and each night she'd read me some of the stories. For a while I wanted to be like her. Sort of eccentric, wearing and doing whatever I liked."

Jackson chuckled at the image of a free-spirited Callie. "And what would that have been?"

"Depends on my age. At one point, a ballerina, of course. I was going to dance *The Nutcracker* in New York for Christmas."

"A noble goal." He was happy to hear her voice perking up.

Callie laughed. "I was eight."

"Precocious, then."

"Next there was the requisite horse phase. I still haven't quite gotten over that," she added wistfully. "And one summer I considered being a missionary."

"What happened to that idea?"

She didn't answer so he glanced over at her. She was blushing. That only made him more curious.

"Come on. Give. What changed your mind?"

"Don't laugh."

"Who's laughing?"

She punched his arm good-naturedly. "I was staying in a different house. The woman was addicted to *Survivor*."

"And?"

"When I saw the kind of conditions they lived in…and it was just for a few weeks." She shuddered. "The dirt. The bugs. Not being able to wash your hair. Not very Christian spirited of me to be turned off doing the Lord's work because of bugs, right? So it's not one of my finer memories."

"We're not all cut out for that kind of thing," Jackson offered, hoping to reassure that he wasn't judging.

"Did you just say I'm not a good Christian?" she teased.

Jackson lifted one hand off the wheel in mock surrender. "I think you're the one who said that. I was just, um, pointing out that you have other good qualities. Teaching kindergarten. That's not for the faint of heart."

"You're sweet, Jackson. I appreciate you trying to cheer me up. You'd think someone who dealt with twenty-five kindergartners on a daily basis could handle more than this."

Jackson reached over and rested his hand on her shoulder; it was the closest he could manage to giving a comforting hug while driving. "I doubt your kindergartners take target practice using you as their target."

Callie laughed her appreciation. "True. They're more likely to attack with sticky fingers."

She waggled her fingers at him and he laughed, but his pulse started racing at the thought of this woman running at him with sticky fingers. Tension suddenly hummed in the air and the car seemed too small for the feelings that were building.

Jackson breathed a sigh of relief when he spied the road sign for a shopping mall ahead. He pointed it out to Callie. "We need a change of clothes."

Callie cheered. "Thank you. Thank you. Thank you. I didn't want to complain, but these clothes are pretty much taking on a life of their own. If I'd known we were heading out on a tour of every back road in America, I'd have packed accordingly."

Her cheerful spirits never failed to lift his own. Turned out Ben's assessment of her had been pretty accurate after all. "You're a good sport, Callie Martin. I don't want to risk going into the mall itself, but we do have to pick up food and supplies. We'll need some warmer clothes for where we're headed."

"We have an actual destination?" Callie joked. "I was beginning to think we were just going to live in assorted rental cars until it was time for the trial."

"Cute, Cal. We've got more than a week until the trial starts. I have something with more legroom in mind."

"My legs thank you. Where are we going that I need more clothes?"

He grinned at her. "It's a surprise."

"Promise me it doesn't come with more real-life action scenes."

Jackson made a face. "I'm hoping for a peaceful few days."

"Somewhere cold." She twirled a strand of hair. "Hmm. Let me guess. The North Pole?"

Jackson struggled to ignore the way she was twisting her hair around her finger. It reminded him a bit too much of how she was starting to twist her way around his heart. He cleared the frog from his throat. "That would help with the Christmas spirit. But, no."

"We could fight off the attackers with an army of elves and misfit toys."

"Peaceful, Callie. Think peaceful thoughts."

Shopping was anything but peaceful. Rather than risk heading into the mall, Jackson had parked around the side so they could go directly into an all-purpose store but even that was crowded this close to Christmas. Chaos reigned, but it was a good chaos, Callie decided. She felt safe. Nothing like hundreds of strangers swarming around in a mad shopping frenzy to help you hide.

She'd probably feel less secure if Jackson hadn't checked in with the sheriff before they left the car. The four men who had been arrested were all still in custody, awaiting charges. A search of their car had turned up a cache of unlicensed weapons, providing excellent grounds for holding them. The fact that the men had no identification on them and had already escaped once had the local officials keeping very tight guard while they waited for the feds to arrive.

So for now she was safe.

Callie didn't plan to dwell on how long that would last. She would live in the moment and be grateful. *Thank You,*

Lord, for saving us and for letting us have this time of peace.

Callie wandered over to a holiday display while Jackson stood in line at the register. She couldn't imagine what destination he had in mind that would require such a boatload of clothing, but she owed him so she'd be a good little witness and play along with his surprise.

While she waited, she watched a mother and her two daughters try to choose from an assortment of ornaments. The little girl seemed to have an eye for all the sparkly purple balls, while the older girl was looking longingly at a tree featuring some trendy boy band. Callie's heart gave a tug as she watched the mother deftly suggest a slightly less gaudy star for the little girl and indulge the older one with a bell from the tree. The older girl threw her arms around her mother, and Callie turned away, fighting back the tears.

She almost walked into Jackson, who had come up behind her. "I wish we had time to linger, Callie."

"You do?" He didn't strike her as the kind to love shopping.

"Let me rephrase. For your sake, I wish it was safe to linger, but we need to keep moving."

"I know." She sniffed back the last of her tears and focused on what she had to be grateful for. "Do we have time for me to pick up some fancy coffee drink for the road?"

She watched Jackson scan the crowd. Maybe he wasn't as confident about their safety as he'd seemed.

"Can you wait a bit? I want to switch out cars again. I noticed a rental place as we came in. There was a coffee shop next to it."

And all she'd noticed were the Christmas decorations. Good thing she wasn't the one in charge of her own security. Trying to shake off a sense of unease, she joked. "What, bullet holes in the trunk cramp your style?"

"Not good for my reputation as most awesome marshal."

Callie smiled at him. "I think you have a lock on that one."

Jackson swallowed hard and turned away. Callie hid a grin. Had she just made Jackson blush?

Once they got the packages in the car and headed over to the rental place, Jackson walked her to the coffee shop. "I'll be back for you. I'm just going to be in the shop doing the paperwork for a new car."

Callie nodded. "What can I get you? My treat. No protests. Think of it as my small way of repaying you."

"You don't need to repay me, Callie. I'm just doing my job."

She wondered who he was trying to convince. "I can still buy you coffee."

He stared at her a long moment, then conceded. "Make mine hot chocolate, please. I'm at the point of never wanting to taste coffee again."

"I hear you. Hot chocolate it is."

"After you get the drinks, wait here. Call if anything concerns you."

She had to ask. "Is there a reason I should expect trouble?"

He closed his eyes a second, as if weighing his words. "In our world, Callie, you should always expect trouble. I'm sorry. That's reality."

Callie tried not to let him see how his words had affected her, causing the sinking feeling that made her lose her appetite for silly Christmas drinks. Apparently she failed.

"It's okay, Callie. You can get the drinks. We have to be careful, but you can't stop living. If you do that, they win as surely as if they got to you. Right now you're as safe as we can hope for. If anyone had gotten away, they'd have called me. I made it really clear we didn't want a surprise like that again."

Callie chuckled despite her fears. "I'm sure you did. Probably had them all running scared."

"I want you safe."

And that was it, the bottom line. "I know." She nibbled on her lip, wondering how much to say. "I feel totally safe when I'm with you. Thank you, Jackson." She impulsively reached up and gave him a quick hug.

Callie headed in to the coffee shop with their conversation heavy on her heart. Her spirits lifted quickly once she stepped through the doorway. Even this tiny chain store was decorated for Christmas. She missed having the opportunity to do that this year. Because the trial wasn't scheduled to occur until after Christmas, she'd planned to get a tree and decorate her New York apartment a little. And New York had been so inspiring. She smiled, thinking that one of the perks of this witness relocation was that she'd gotten to see the sights of New York at Christmas. She'd spent a lot of time wandering around the city on her own. Skating at Rockefeller Center was her favorite experience. Pretty cool stuff for the girl from Texas.

But here she was now, days before Christmas and she felt more a kindred spirit with Mary and Joseph, far from home with no place to stay. But she had no family or child. All she had was one big pity party going on in her head, taunting her with memories of all she'd lost.

Which meant it was time to remind herself of what she had to be grateful for, starting with one amazing and handsome marshal who was bent on keeping her alive. Time to shake off the self-pity and be happy to have him and that she was still alive.

By the time Callie reached the front of the line, received their drinks and headed to the door to meet Jackson, she'd gotten herself back under control. God had a purpose for her, and she would follow it, whatever it was and wherever He led her.

Jackson was pacing outside the door. Maybe he wasn't quite as relaxed as he'd had her believe. Callie hastened her steps and pushed her back against the door to open it. Then stopped cold.

"Jackson, it's snowing."

"Yeah, all the more reason to get going. The forecast is for a few inches."

"Really?" Callie twirled, sticking her tongue out to catch a snowflake. "I've never seen real snow before—only in the movies or on TV. It's so pretty."

"It will be prettier where we're going. Let's get started."

"What color car do we have this time."

He grinned. "Green."

A huge smile burst across her face. "You rented us a green car for Christmas?"

He winked. "It will blend in better with the trees."

"You can't fool me, Jackson Walker. Little by little I'm winning you over to the Christmas spirit."

He bit his lip as he opened the door for her. "Let me take the drinks while you get in."

Callie handed over the tray, then ducked into the car. She stopped the second she saw the interior and popped back out. "No way! You didn't! Tell me you didn't just do this."

Jackson's wide grin told her he had indeed.

"Jackson, you sweetheart! You gave me Christmas. It's amazing!" Little white lights twinkled around the car's interior. Garlands were draped along the windows and across the back. A mini–artificial tree sat on the backseat, and Christmas music spilled from the CD player.

She swirled herself around and into his arms and

planted a kiss on his cheek. "You are the sweetest man ever. Thank you. Thank you. Thank you."

He smiled gently back at her. "You're welcome."

"How did you manage it?"

"I bought it earlier. I put it up when you took a really long time in the coffee shop," he teased.

"There was a line."

"That's fine. It gave me plenty of time. But now it's getting late. Can we get back on the road?"

Callie climbed in and inhaled deeply. The car smelled so good, like a pine forest. "What's the smell?" she asked Jackson when he came around and got in the driver's side.

He pointed to the bag wedged under the front dashboard. "Open it."

Callie picked up the bag and opened it carefully. She peeked inside and gasped. Burying her face in the bag, she inhaled deeply of the fragrant pine-scented candles. She knew tears were glistening in her eyes when she looked up to thank Jackson, but she didn't care.

"You bought these in the store, too?"

His voice was soft when he answered. "Yes. While you were staring at the mother and her children."

Callie took a deep breath. She hadn't known he'd been watching her. She should feel embarrassed, but something about Jackson's gesture removed that restraint. She was simply overwhelmed.

"You're a very special man, Jackson. No one has ever done anything like this for me. You've gone above and beyond. Thank you."

The warmth of his smile stirred deep in her heart.

"Making you happy is fun. I wish I could have seen you with your class. You're like a big kid."

She sighed wistfully. "The kids would adore this. I used

to love seeing their faces the first time they came in after I decorated the classroom."

"I think I know the feeling. That was some squeal." His grin told her he had enjoyed it almost as much as she had.

Callie settled back into her seat, contentedly sipping her mint-flavored mocha latte, listening to the soft music and watching the snow gently coat the car and road. These moments were proof enough that God was good and life was worth celebrating. You could build a life snatching small moments like these so long as you took the time to appreciate them and give thanks.

"All we've done is talk about me," Callie said as she drained the last drop of her coffee. "What about you? What kinds of memories do you have?"

He didn't answer right away so Callie looked over to see what had distracted him. "Jackson?"

She saw his fingers tighten on the wheel and his face take on a stark expression. Had she said something wrong?

"I'm sorry. That was insensitive of me. Do you usually spend the holidays with your family?" She hesitated a moment as a thought came to her. "Won't they miss you if you're here with me for Christmas?"

The intensity of his silence should have warned her.

"I don't have any family."

Her brow furrowed. "All this time I've been talking about me...I didn't think to ask about your family. Were you an orphan, too?"

"If you can call losing your family at eighteen being an orphan."

Callie gasped. "Oh, Jackson." She reached out to him, but his shoulder felt so rigid. She squeezed gently and whispered. "I'm so sorry for your loss."

He didn't respond. His posture and the sudden eerie

calm that had descended over him told her there was much more to the story.

"Do you want to tell me what happened?"

"They were murdered." Silence stretched as the harsh words hung between them. "Please don't ask. I don't talk about it. Ever."

His voice sounded stark, raw. Callie recoiled, unsure how to respond. Finally she reached over to shut off the Christmas CD. The festive music, the twinkling lights, the garland—what had seemed joyous moments before—now seemed glaringly inappropriate.

Jackson put his hand out to stop her. "That's okay, Callie. I don't want to spoil your enjoyment. It's just not something I talk about."

NINE

After hours of driving with no sign of trouble, Jackson began to relax—slightly. He wouldn't let down his guard, but hopefully in ditching their tail, they'd made it safely away and could hide out until the trial without any further trouble.

Something needed to change. These days of constant tension and running were taking a visible toll on Callie. Of course he wanted her alive to testify, but he wanted her spirit to survive also. He wanted her to be able to live without fear.

As he was thinking that, Jackson realized he'd mostly come around to believing in her innocence. The more he got to know her, the less he worried about her involvement. Now he worried about her future. She'd had to give up everything that made her who she was. What would she do for work?

That wasn't his concern. His job was to get her safely to trial, not to obsess about what happened next. But being alone together in confined spaces for so many hours had begun to encourage a different relationship than he usually had with witnesses. He wanted good things for Callie. She deserved them. At least the Callie he thought he knew deserved them. There was still a tiny kernel of doubt that warned him not to trust too deeply, but it was losing strength with each passing day.

A person couldn't fake the good heart she showed. She truly cared about people. That didn't jibe with her being part of the drug gang.

He'd thought Ben was getting soft. Time to rein himself in and focus on the job. The fact that he was even thinking such things was a complete departure from protocol and from his norm. So be it. He would stay focused, but no harm would come from being kind to a person who needed care for a few days. So long as he didn't let his guard down in any personal way to her. Which meant he had no intention of answering her unspoken questions about his family. As he'd warned her, he didn't discuss it. Or allow himself to consciously think about it, though the memory was never very far away. It couldn't be. That one incident had made him who he was today—the good and the bad.

Because Callie was curled up in the backseat asleep, Jackson took one last chance to check in with the sheriff in Ohio before committing to their new destination.

Once he had assurances that all was quiet, the men were still locked up and no one had shown up to bail them out, Jackson decided it was safe to stop. He turned off the highway to the small Vermont town he'd been aiming for. If Callie wanted a true Christmas, there was no better place to find it than Millers Creek, Vermont.

Jackson knew the town from his college years, and it was far enough off the beaten track that they wouldn't be easily found. Millers Creek wasn't exactly a hotbed of drug trafficking.

He'd worked there with his college roommate the summer after his freshman year, when his family was still alive and life was full of promise.

He'd come back again to mourn after his family was

murdered. There was something soothing in the quiet rhythms of life in this farm town. People were real and kind. He'd come close to putting roots down here. Until he discovered he was the kind of person who didn't put down roots.

The murders had severed all the ties that grounded him. They'd cut him loose to become a restless wanderer. He'd joined the army for a while, tried his hand at school and eventually ended up in the Marshals Service.

Now he'd be back in Millers Creek. It was fitting he take Callie there, a fellow lost soul seeking some way of holding her own in a harsh world. He hoped she'd find the peace of the season in his favorite town. He'd come up with the idea when she started him thinking about Christmas. He remembered being there the December after his world had crashed. All around him people were celebrating the season with simple joy. He'd been too mired in his own grief to want any part of it then, but he knew it was exactly what Callie needed now.

Night had fallen as they drove, and it was too late to go into town. He'd save that surprise for another day. Tonight he just wanted to get her fed and tucked safely in bed. He reached over the seat divider and tapped her leg. "Callie, time to wake up."

"What? Why?"

He caught her image in his rearview mirror. "You're going to want to see this. We're almost there."

She uncurled and stretched, and Jackson kept his eyes firmly on the road to avoid staring. The sight of her emerging from sleep, heavy eyed and yawning, stirred the very feelings he was fighting to tamp down.

"Are you finally going to tell me where 'there' is?"

"Vermont." He hoped she didn't detect the clipped tone.

"Vermont." Callie repeated as she rubbed at her tired eyes. "That's a long way from Texas."

"It is, but they have airports. We can fly you right in for the trial."

"I didn't mean it that way. I was just thinking that this witness protection gig has me seeing more places than I ever dreamed. Maybe that should be your motto. Join WITSEC, and see the country."

She stretched and rubbed her eyes again. "Sorry, I'm just a little giddy." She crawled over the seat divider and settled into the seat beside him.

"You're cute when you're giddy."

Callie started to laugh. Jackson looked on quizzically.

"You just reminded me of my favorite line from the old movie, when Clarice tells Rudolph he's cute and he dances around singing."

He smiled. "I remember. Haven't thought of that movie in years." He turned the car down the tree-lined lane to the cabins. If she was excited now, wait until she saw what awaited them. Anticipating her reaction made him feel slightly giddy himself. He considered trying to squash the feeling. US marshals were supposed to be serious. But given the day they'd had, starting with the car chase and ending up with a six-hundred-mile drive, he figured he was entitled to a little frivolity.

Snow was still falling lightly when he pulled up in front of the main building. "Do you want to wait here or come with me?"

A smile lit her face. "I'm coming. Is this the surprise?"

He nodded and they got out of the car.

Callie closed her eyes and inhaled deeply. She gave a contented sigh. "It's lovely."

"Even in the dark?"

"Especially in the dark. I don't need light to smell the

pine trees. They're amazing. Look at how the snow is drifting down and just resting on the branches. And the lights. I love all the tiny white lights."

They stepped into the lobby of the lodge and Callie's smile grew wider. "Can we just camp out right here?"

He had to agree it sounded like a great idea. A roaring fire in the huge fieldstone fireplace threw a blanket of heat across the room. An instrumental Christmas song played softly through unseen speakers, and a towering pine tree dominated the room from its place in the window. Evergreen boughs hung in swags from the balcony, and everywhere tiny white lights twinkled.

"This is amazing. I hope we can stay here until the trial."

Jackson hoped so, too. It was nice to be back. He'd worked here at the lodge that long-ago summer, so this was a homecoming of sorts.

Once they'd checked in, Jackson called to Callie to head back to the car. Her face fell. "We're not staying here?"

Jackson hid his smile. "We have someplace even better."

She looked doubtful but climbed willingly into the car. Jackson took off down the road that curved along the lake. As they drove, the cabins became spaced farther and farther apart.

Finally he pulled into the driveway of a lakeside cabin at the end of a cul-de-sac. When he'd made their reservation, he'd requested an outdoor light be left lit, and it provided a wonderful view of their cabin.

"Oh, wow. Wow. This is amazing." Callie gushed as she pressed her face against the windshield. "If this is witness protection, I don't ever want to be found." Her happy laugh wound its way right into Jackson's heart.

He laughed along with her, delighted to see her so happy. And she hadn't even seen the inside yet. From what he remembered, the interiors were always exquisitely designed, but when he reserved the cabin, he'd put in a special request for a few Christmas decorations, if possible.

"I need for you to wait in the car while I check out the cabin."

Callie seemed surprised. "Is that really necessary?"

"Necessary to check? Absolutely. Do I expect to find anything? No. I expect this to be totally clean and safe. But then we thought the New York office was safe, too, and you know how that turned out."

"You never relax, do you?"

He could ask her to explain the question, but he knew what she meant. "Not if it means your safety. There's a time for relaxing. It's not the same thing as being careless."

"That must be a difficult way to live."

He shrugged it off. It wasn't something he thought much about. Maybe because he didn't know any other life. "We all make choices. You made the choice to testify."

"I did. I have to admit, though, I had no idea what I was getting myself into."

"Do you regret it?"

He could see her chewing on his question. "Am I sorry my life was turned on its head? I am. Do I regret agreeing to testify? No. Those men need to be stopped from hurting anyone else."

"Then you understand. Sometimes the choice isn't the one that makes life easy. But you do it because it's right."

Callie nodded slowly as if she were contemplating what he'd said. She finally reached over to place her hand on his arm. "Thank you for choosing to keep me alive and safe. And thank you for finding this place and giving me this time."

Jackson couldn't get out of the car fast enough. Every time she started praising him, he got more uncomfortable. He was doing his job. That was all.

Was it? Or was he deluding himself? Either way, it had to stop. This was a job. Nothing more. He'd just keep telling himself that. He drew his gun and headed for the cabin door.

He didn't expect there to be a problem here. They'd made a clean getaway and there was no reason anyone would have heard his reservation call. He'd used a fake name anyway, hoping that he wouldn't encounter anyone who might recall the youth who'd worked here more than a decade ago. If they did, he'd cover, but that wasn't his concern now. He needed to play it safe and scope the entire cabin.

A quick walk-through yielded nothing suspicious. The resort staff had outdone themselves decorating the cabin. Callie would be thrilled. Imagining her reaction, Jackson was just turning for the door to call her when a sharp crack sounded from the woods. Jackson raised his gun and rushed toward the door.

From the porch, he couldn't see Callie in the car. Panic burned in his throat and he broke into a cold sweat. Forcibly restraining himself from blindly running out, Jackson stood in the shelter of the porch and let his gaze search the woods for any sign of movement.

How in the world could they have been tracked here? He'd done everything imaginable to make sure there was no way to be followed. Except...

Jackson felt a little sick. He hadn't wanted to alert the office to his plans, just in case... He couldn't even finish the thought. Didn't want to actually put it into words. That was giving too much credence to the possibility that someone he worked with couldn't be trusted.

Jackson sensed motion in the woods off to his right, so he ducked down behind a post on the porch and slowly scanned the landscape. The new fallen snow lent a brightness to the night and the clouds were starting to clear. He could make out the trees, but all was still. Had whoever was out there seen him?

Whoever they were, at least he knew they hadn't grabbed Callie yet. The only sound he'd heard had been from the woods. There had been no noise of a car door opening or closing. He hadn't heard any sound from Callie either and he knew she wouldn't go silently. She must be hiding in the front seat. He wanted to call out to her for reassurance but couldn't risk alerting the enemy.

Jackson crouched there waiting, wondering. Had he been seen? It made sense that the person or persons who were out there had watched him enter the house. How long would they wait before making a move?

Just when Jackson was beginning to debate the wisdom of trying to reach Callie, another sound echoed through the night, a series of crackles, as if some creature was scrambling through the underbrush.

Seconds later a bear lumbered out from the tree line, paused, sniffed the air and looked around the clearing. Jackson slumped back against the house. For the first time in his life, he was relieved to see a wild animal. He didn't like that it had turned and was headed toward the car and Callie, but he could scare it off. Better this than human predators.

Jackson fired a shot into the air. The bear lifted his head, sniffed and turned back into the woods. Jackson waited a few minutes after the bear had crashed out of sight before easing down the steps. He didn't want his actions to encourage a return visit.

As soon as he reached the opposite side of the car, Jackson slouched down and grabbed for the door handle. When he opened the door, the sudden flare of light revealed Callie huddled under the dashboard. Good. She'd shown a natural instinct to hide rather than run. Jackson reached to help her up, taking care to keep an eye out in case the bear returned. "Are you okay?"

"What happened?"

"There was a bear. I fired a shot to scare it off."

"A bear?" She burst out laughing.

Okay, he'd seen people react oddly to stress before. "Callie? Come on. Let's get you into the house so you can calm down."

She only laughed harder. "I know this is stress release I'm feeling, but honestly, Jackson, you've got to admit it's pretty funny."

He really wasn't sure what was funny about a bear coming at her and he said so.

"It's funny because it's only a bear, and you and I both probably had the same reaction to hearing that branch snap. You thought they'd found us again, didn't you?"

"I did." Tension tightened his jaw just remembering his instant reaction. Recalling the men he'd been too willing to blame.

"And I'm sure you were relieved to see the bear."

He nodded, beginning to see where she was going.

"Who in their right mind is relieved to be confronted by a bear?"

Jackson shook his head. "You're one of a kind, Cal. One of a kind. Let me get you inside, then I'll unpack."

Callie reached for her bags. "If I help, we'll be done half as fast. And one of us can keep watch in case our friend returns."

Jackson started to protest, but she was already marching up the path, arms loaded with their purchases. He grabbed a couple of bags and started up after her.

* * *

Callie rested her bags down on the porch so she could have a hand free to open the door. Bear or no bear, she almost didn't want to go inside. The porch was so peaceful. Imagine what it must be like to sit out here on a summer evening. She inhaled the cold, clean air and for the first time in days felt the stress begin to ease. It seemed Jackson had found the perfect place for her to hide away.

Those feelings were confirmed as she opened the door into a winter wonderland. A trio of Christmas trees clustered in the corner perfumed the air with a fresh pine scent. Tiny white lights edged the ceiling and looped along the far wall. Callie gasped as she headed over to the wall of sheer glass. Jackson wasn't going to be happy about that, but she was. The snow lent an eerie white glow to the night and she could see the lake. Outside lights graced the trees closer to the house and lit a pathway down to the lake.

"Thank You, Lord. Thank You for this special place to celebrate the peace and love of Your son's birth."

She turned around to find Jackson watching her. She gave him a quick smile. "Just talking to God again."

He nodded. "One of these days you'll have to tell me about that. But now, if it's all the same to you, I think we should get settled in and get some sleep."

Callie agreed, though she doubted either of them would sleep much. He needed to because he'd done all the driving while she'd napped. Would he? From what she'd observed so far, there wasn't much chance.

She waited until they'd finished touring the cabin and were ready to turn in before offering her help. "Jackson, I think I'm beginning to understand what you mean about never being able to relax, never being completely sure you're safe."

He stopped drawing the drapes across the lake window. He lowered his arms and crossed them as he turned to look at her. "What brought this on?"

"The bear. I know he wasn't really a danger to us, not like the guys who are after me, but the way we reacted to him, the immediate surge of adrenaline and the fear they'd found us again, that doesn't leave, does it? It becomes a new way of life."

He stood there, arms crossed, staring down at his feet for a long moment before answering. "That's my reality. For you, it should gradually get better. We have witnesses who have been in the program a long time. Some eventually feel safe enough to withdraw. The person who was after them either dies or goes to prison. Whatever, they feel the threat is removed. For others, WITSEC becomes a way of life. But I'm told, even for them, eventually the urgency wears off. Little by little you stop looking over your shoulder. It takes time, though."

She nodded. "Thanks, I think. I'll try to remember that. But I meant in a more immediate way. You don't ever really get time off, do you? There's no one else to relieve you. I know it's because of how we had to run, how we have to keep changing direction. But this has to be hard on you. You need sleep."

"I've learned to do without."

"You're supposed to be protecting me, but since it's just the two of us, we could take turns being on watch. That way you'd get to sleep once in a while."

He didn't laugh outright. She gave him credit for that, but she could see he didn't like her idea.

"No offense, Callie, but you're not trained as a body-guard or anything, are you?"

"No, but I am used to being responsible for a class of five-year-olds. That certainly teaches you observation skills. I'm not saying I'd be able to fight off an attack, but

I can at least keep watch if you need me to. I've had plenty of time to sleep in the car. I can stay up awhile if you want to catch a nap."

"Thanks, Cal. I really mean that. I appreciate you thinking of me." He gave her a quick hug. "I'm a light sleeper, and we should be plenty safe here. I don't think there's anything to worry about."

"Okay." She fiddled with an ornament on the tree. "How long do you expect us to stay here?"

"I'd like to stay until we have to head in for trial, but until I know how they keep tracking us, I can't be sure."

"Okay. Good night, then."

She turned to head into the room he'd shown her.

"Callie?"

She turned back, glad for the chance to talk a few more minutes. "Yes?"

"Are you comfortable alone here with me? I don't want to keep you isolated if it bothers you. It just seems safest."

He waited for her response. There was tension in the way he held himself, as if her answer really mattered, so she gave the question serious thought. Comfortable was a good word to describe how she felt with him—if she was talking safety. But the marshal unsettled her, too. Being with him was exciting, intriguing, even fun at times. But comfortable? Not if she allowed herself to think how much she was growing to like him. Those kinds of thoughts could have her end up with a broken heart.

"I'm fine. Whatever you think is best. I don't want to be a burden."

He studied her for what felt like a long time. Then he nodded. "Okay. Tell me if it changes."

She was almost to her door, and his words were so soft, she wasn't sure she was meant to hear them, but they rested lightly on her heart. "You're never a burden."

TEN

After two days of hanging out together in the cabin, the novelty had worn thin and the idea of spending more time cooped up like this lay heavy. Callie was getting restless, and that worried Jackson. Restless people took foolish risks. She was puttering around in the kitchen, so Jackson headed there. "Cal, we need to talk."

She eyed him with an expression of fear. "Did they get away?"

"What? Oh, no. Nothing along those lines."

"Please don't scare me like that." She wiped the sparkling clean counter with the sponge, scrubbing at an invisible spot. Probably to avoid looking at him.

"Callie."

She looked up and he saw the tears glistening in her eyes.

"What's wrong?"

"Nothing." She waved him away. "I'm just feeling emotional."

He figured he had a pretty good idea why. It was Christmas Eve, and she was locked away in a lonely cabin in the middle of nowhere. He wished he could take her out someplace fancy, but he didn't dare. That would have been one of those foolish risks he wanted to warn her about.

"I guess I'll just go read or something until it's time to eat."

The dejection was so clear in her voice, but he knew what he could say to bring a smile back to her lips. "We should have an early dinner."

"Really? I guess you can eat without me. I'm still stuffed from lunch."

"What if I told you the reason was so we could attend the Candlelight Christmas Eve service in town?"

Delight lit Callie's eyes so they sparkled like sapphires. "Really? You would do that for me?"

He poured himself a cup of coffee from the ever-ready pot and gestured to see if she wanted one. When she shook her head, he settled onto one of the kitchen stools. "It's not such a hardship. Once upon a time Christmas services were the most important part of my Christmas celebration. My parents made a point of teaching us the true meaning of Christmas."

Callie turned the burner on and began to boil water for tea. "Can I ask how you fell away?"

Jackson sipped his coffee before setting the mug on the counter. He leaned back, elbows behind him on the counter as he tried to figure out how to explain something that wasn't clear even to him. "I guess I'm your stereotypical caricature of a lapsed Christian. I was a teenager when my parents died. They'd always attended church, but they weren't particularly zealous. Religion was more something we did on Sundays than something we felt all the time. When I was away at college, it began to play even less a part in my life. I'm not sure why really. It just happened. Maybe it was the influence of being away from home with other teens who didn't practice their faith, if they even had one.

"Then my parents died." He paused. "I could say I reacted out of pain, angry at God for having two good people taken from this Earth, but that wouldn't be truthful. Honestly, I'm sort of embarrassed to admit it, but religion wasn't a big enough part of my life by then for me to even think about blaming God for taking my family. I was angry, but at the people who shot them and the people who wouldn't testify against the killers."

He shifted uncomfortably and stepped off the chair so he could pace. "Later, the army chaplain tried to encourage me to strive for inner peace to help me during battle and downtime. I was still too pumped full of anger and even hatred."

"What changed?"

He shrugged. "It didn't change so much as weaken. I got older, learned to temper my emotions, not get so carried away by my own importance in the universe."

He intended the last to lighten the mood and it succeeded. Callie smiled at him.

"You are important to God."

"You sound so sure of that." That certainty left him sad. It must be comforting to have such faith. If only he were capable.

"I am. Now. I wasn't always."

Callie's words knocked Jackson out of his sullen funk. Faith seemed such an integral part of her. It was hard to imagine a Callie not confident in it. "Seriously? Tell."

"Not now. It's a long story and not really what I want to be thinking of on Christmas Eve."

"Okay. I'll accept that. But I do want to hear it sometime. If someone as faith filled as you wasn't always that way, maybe there's hope for the rest of us."

"There's always hope, Jackson. That's the whole point of the Savior being born on Christmas Day." She reached up and laid a hand to his cheek, as if seeking the closeness that touch brought. "Thank you for thinking of this, for going out of your way to make me happy. All of this, all that you've done, it's so far above and beyond. I can't even express my thanks sufficiently. So I'll say this—I'll pray for you."

Jackson was truly humbled by her words.

"You're an amazing person, Callie Martin." If only he had the right to say the rest of his thoughts aloud. That in his deepest heart he wished she wasn't in witness protection and that they had met under different circumstances. Because if he could, if they had a chance, he might find himself starting to believe in that hope of hers.

Moonlight glistened on a fresh coat of snow as Jackson and Callie strolled up the path to the tiny country church. Organ music floated on the air and light from the church spilled through stained glass windows, creating a multicolored patchwork on the pristine snow banks. The church was truly a beacon in the cold night, a light for the lost.

At least that's how Jackson felt as he rested his hand on the small of Callie's back and guided her through the doorway.

How many years had it been since he'd last stepped foot into a sacred space? They entered the foyer, and as the gentle music and a sense of peace encircled him, welcoming him home, he knew it had been too long.

Jackson chose a pew in the back, in the shadows so as not to attract attention or recognition. They sat side by side in quiet harmony, listening as the readings recounted the Christmas story. Candlelight and Christmas hymns wove a peaceful cocoon. There was no tension, no fear—just joy for the good news of the Savior's birth.

Callie's voice rose with the congregation as they sang the final hymn of joy. Then, in silent accord, the two of them waited for the bulk of the crowd to leave before making their way outside.

Snow was falling again, drifting gracefully around them as they walked back to the car. Callie smiled and spun slowly around in it. "Christmas snow. It's perfect." She leaned into him to express her thanks. "How ironic that I'm running for my life, because I've never felt so peaceful on Christmas." She kissed her fingertips and brushed them against his cheek. "Thank you for doing this for me."

"I should be thanking you for inspiring me to go." Jackson's voice went husky with a multitude of emotions. "It was...special."

They stood for a long moment in the silent night. He rested his arm around her shoulder and drew her closer, then reached to brush a snowflake from her hair. His fingers lingered, stroking her hair. "Ah, Callie girl." He leaned down until their lips were almost touching, until he could look deeply into her eyes. His finger traced along the side of her cheek. Church bells chimed as he leaned closer, brushing his lips across hers. "Merry Christmas, Callie."

Emotions ran deep as they huddled together in the cold air. Did she feel this connection between them? Was she as perplexed by it as he was? He thought she felt it, too. A part of him longed to ask, but it was a futile question. Why torture them both with acknowledgment of something that could never be? Better to simply enjoy the unexpected blessing of this short time out of time.

"I enjoyed your singing," he said, attempting to recover his balance. "Your voice is made for church music."

"Thanks. This is the first time I've sung since...well, since that night. I've missed it. Besides, it's hard to go wrong with hymns."

"You only say that because you haven't heard me sing," Jackson retorted.

"Oh, come on. You can't be that bad."

"My younger brother once threatened to report me to Santa if I sang. He said my singing put me on the naughty list."

Callie laughed, but quickly they both fell silent, realizing he'd spoken of his family. He gave her credit for not pushing more.

They walked the rest of the distance to the car in silence. Jackson held the door for her.

When she was settled, he leaned down into the open doorway. "Cal, you're right I did this for you, but it was a blessing for me, as well. I haven't been to Christmas services since my parents died. I'm glad we went and that I had you to share it with."

Not surprisingly, sleep didn't come easily. Jackson tossed and turned for an hour before resigning himself to another sleepless night. He rose and went out to the living room. The air was cold, so he stirred up the embers and added logs to the fire.

For safety's sake, he'd drawn the heavy drapes across the glass wall, but now he pulled them back enough that he could stare out at the expanse of snow and frozen lake. Sometimes he felt as though his entire being was as frozen as the landscape. He'd dealt with grief by closing himself off. Ice was numbing, and it was easier to deal when you felt nothing. He'd become so good at it, he hadn't even been aware anymore.

Until Callie.

Her warmth was thawing his heart. It hurt.

Where once there had been nothing, now he felt the stirrings of feelings. Church had dredged up so many memories.

Looking out at the frigid water, Jackson fell back in

time, remembering how he used to race his brother across the icy lake by their house. His brother had planned to play professional hockey, and it had irked him that Jackson could beat him across the lake. Even though he had been two years younger, Sam had been intent on besting his big brother. He'd practiced and practiced. That last weekend when he'd been home, Sam had challenged him to a race—and won. Just thinking of it now brought waves of loss that bowed Jackson over. He instinctively pulled in on himself, curling his body inward to protect against the pain.

It was useless. Once opened, memories came flooding in. Other Christmases. Presents piled under the tree; his father going ahead to make sure Santa was gone before the boys came down. Playing with their new toys on Christmas morning. Later, when they were older, challenging each other to marathon video-game matches. He and Sam had been best buddies as well as brothers. Losing his parents had been bad enough, but losing Sam… Jackson sucked in a breath. He'd thought he would die, too.

Even without seeing or hearing a sound, Jackson knew the minute Callie entered the room behind him. He felt her presence, and his body involuntarily stiffened. Part of him welcomed her company as a respite from his thoughts, but his pride hoped she would read his body language and go away. It was hard enough to fight the memories on his own. He didn't want her witnessing his struggle.

And there he went repeating old patterns, cutting off all the people who could help. Too bad. It was the only way he knew to survive. And Callie wasn't here to help him. It was his job to protect her.

Rigid, he waited until he felt her retreat, then he donned his coat and headed outside. He hadn't experienced the relief he'd expected when she withdrew. Loneliness invaded his heart, replacing the warmth she brought. Perhaps cold air would put his memories back where they belonged and help him rebuild his armor.

Callie heard the door close and walked back into the living room. She hadn't wanted to disturb Jackson before, but there had been such a profound sadness emanating from him that it was all she could do not to rush forward. She'd retreated to pray for him. Maybe that had been a mistake. Maybe she should have gone forward and prayed with him instead.

She walked over to where he had drawn back the curtains. Hiding behind one side, she could watch his progress down to the lake. When he reached the shore, he just stood there. What was he thinking? Was he troubled by the case, or were his problems more personal?

He looked so alone.

On the surface, that sounded silly. Obviously he was alone. But this went deeper. He gave off the sense of a man who had been by himself a long time. A man who might not know any other way to be. From what little she'd seen, he depended on no one, got close to no one. She had the strongest urge to reach out, to offer comfort.

It would be rejected. She knew that instinctively.

She stood for a long time, watching him watch the lake. When finally he turned to come inside, she pulled back behind the curtain and headed to her bedroom. She'd give him his privacy, and she'd pray for the Lord to show her how to reach him.

ELEVEN

The mouth-watering aroma of coffee brewing drew Callie from her dreams several hours later. She stretched and took a moment to remember where she was.

Christmas morning. Joy flooded her being. This was a day she'd expected to be so sad, but Jackson had changed that. He'd gone to so much effort. Thinking back to last night, she realized he'd done it at great personal cost. She blinked back tears of gratitude. Today she would find a way to make it up to him.

Rising with a heart full of anticipation, Callie sifted through her duffel looking for something appropriate to wear. There wasn't much in the way of holiday clothing, but she dug out a green sweater to go with her flannel-lined jeans. The plaid lining was festive anyway. The red ribbon on her stuffed penguin's neck caught her eye so she borrowed it to tie back her hair.

By the time Callie arrived in the kitchen, delicious food aromas mingled with the scent of freshly brewed coffee. She sniffed the air, then peeked under the skillet cover. "Bacon and pancakes? Jackson Walker, you are some kind of culinary superhero." She reached up and kissed his cheek. "Merry Christmas."

He smiled back at her, and there was almost no trace

of the lonely man from last night. Shadows under his eyes reflected the loss of sleep, but those eyes were twinkling and his smile was happy. "One superhero-designed breakfast coming up."

They ate in silence, each a little awkward after their near kiss the previous night. Finally Jackson made a suggestion. "How about getting outside today?"

"Hmm?"

He smiled softly. Callie's coffee hadn't kicked in yet.

"Forecast is for a beautiful day. We've been cooped up inside the car and here for days. How about we go skiing?"

Callie swallowed another sip of coffee. "You ski?"

"I have. You don't spend time in Vermont without learning how. But I don't mean downhill. Let's grab some cross-country skis and go out and see the area."

She set her coffee on the counter and sleepily rubbed her eyes. "Um, okay. I guess I could do that."

"Where's that Texas can-do attitude?"

"Still in bed."

Jackson laughed. "You finish your coffee and have some breakfast. I'll go down to the lodge and rent us some skis." And check in with his office.

By the time he returned, she was dressed and ready to go. He gave her some extra layers he'd picked up in the ski shop but held back the information he'd also acquired. No need to start her Christmas day off badly with the news that the trial had been postponed a week.

Truth be told, the idea of spending an extra week holed away here with Callie scared him more than the thought of bringing her in for trial. They might be spending quite a bit of time outside to bolster his willpower. Thankfully backup would be arriving tomorrow. Keeping his distance would be easier with additional marshals in the house.

So today, he'd allow himself to enjoy her company—from a safe distance.

There might be something to that Texas bravado after all, Jackson decided as the day went on. Callie turned out to be a natural athlete with a terrific aptitude for skiing. They spent hours in the woods, skiing along paths and coasting over fresh snow. She seemed to thrive on the cold, fresh air and sunlight. Her cheeks were rosy and her eyes sparkling by the time he decided they should head back.

Her good humor proved infectious, and his own spirits were high, so he suggested they stop for a quick lunch at the lodge before heading back to their cabin.

Jackson suggested calling for a lodge shuttle as they finished the meal and left the lodge.

Callie objected. "I can't believe I'm saying this after skiing all morning, but I'm stuffed. Can we walk a bit and then ski back?"

"Sure." Jackson retrieved their skis from where he'd checked them at the door. Slinging them over his shoulder, he joined Callie. "Let's go along the shore. The ice is frozen solid and we can actually walk on the lake."

Jackson felt the vibration of his phone as they set off along the far shore. Looking at Callie's happy face, not wanting to spoil her day, he let it go to voice mail.

"Jackson, look! That is so cool. What are they doing?"

Jackson looked up and grinned. "Those are ice boats. They're sailing over the ice. It is pretty cool."

"I so want to try that."

She constantly amazed him. In the midst of all they were going through, she hadn't lost her adventuresome spirit. "I'll see what I can arrange." While she was absorbed in watching the boats, he typed in his password and listened to his voice mail. He ground his teeth as the message sucked the joy from his day, especially when he thought of how his news was going to dampen Callie's spirit. He had no choice but to tell her.

"Callie."

She turned, and the look on her face told him she'd correctly read his expression. "They found us again, didn't they?"

"I'm not sure. I asked an old friend to be on the lookout for anyone new in town who looked like they didn't belong."

"And?"

"She just left me a voice message. Men in a big black car. Nothing to indicate businessmen, and no sign of families."

Callie bit her lip. He could see her fighting back tears. "They don't sound like tourists."

Jackson agreed. One of the reasons he'd decided to come here was knowing he could probably find people from his past who would serve as an early detection system. It sounded like the plan had worked.

"I don't want to take the time to call her for details. Let's continue back to the cabin—slowly and carefully—get what we need and get out of here."

"Okay." He saw the wistful expression she tried to hide, knew she was even more disappointed than he was that their time here had been cut short. And he hadn't even told her about the trial postponement. Knowing the men had tracked them here made him even more curious about the cause of postponement. Were they planning something that required time to get to Callie? He was a professional, so the feeling he had in the pit of his stomach couldn't be terror. But it sure felt like it.

Knowing they'd be sitting ducks walking along the lakeshore, Jackson drew Callie into the shelter of the trees. "We need to hike back through the forest. I don't want to risk being out in the open."

The closer they got to the cabin, the more carefully Jackson proceeded. "Let's go around from behind, just to make sure. There's a hill that overlooks the cabin. We'll be able to see from there."

"How do you know all this?"

"I scoped it out the day after we arrived. Doesn't pay to get caught unawares."

They cautiously made their way up the hill, ducking from tree to tree. Jackson reached the top first. As she came up behind him, he grabbed her arm and pulled her under the full branches of a tall fir tree.

She looked up at him, eyes wide with fright. "They're there?"

He nodded. "There's a car parked by the road. Three men are circling the cabin." He decided not to mention the guns. Anger tugged at his gut. "They should not have found us. No one knew we were here." Except the people in his office. And Callie.

Callie started to say something, so he laid a finger on her lips. "Shh." He whispered in her ear. "Sound carries far."

He kept her pressed close against him, offering a comfort he was far from feeling. "Do you have anything in that cabin that you can't live without?"

Callie started to shake her head. "Well, my Bible." She mouthed the words so they were barely audible. "But I can get another if we can't get that one back. Everything else that really matters is in my backpack." She indicated the bag slung over her shoulders.

"You have your wallet, ID?" he pressed.

"I've learned to go nowhere without them."

"Good." He nodded his approval. "Now, how are you feeling about those skis?"

She eyed him quizzically. "That would matter now because…?"

"We're going to ski out of here."

"You're kidding me," Callie whispered. "No, you're not. Why?"

"They have the road blocked. See that glint off to the right?"

She looked hard, squinting against the sun. "You mean over beyond those trees?"

"Yes. That's the road. See those men pacing along the road? They're not the snow-removal crew."

Callie sank down against the tree trunk. "I wish it had never stopped snowing."

The look she turned on him tore at his heart. "Why do they want me so badly, Jackson?" she whispered. "What don't I understand about this?"

He didn't want to waste any time, but she needed emotional strength if she was going to make it through the journey ahead. He sank beside her in the snow, grateful for the ski pants that protected them from the cold and wetness. "I got an email from John Logan this morning. It said the trial has been postponed a week. He didn't say why. From the manpower they've sent here, I'm guessing your testimony is all that's holding the case against them together."

Tears sparkled on her lashes as she bravely fought them back. "I want this over with. They need to pay." She closed her eyes, and from the look on her face, Jackson suspected she was talking to God again. When she opened her eyes, her strength was back. It was amazing, really, how she drew such power from prayer.

"Let's do this. How are we getting out of here?"

"If we can ski back over those hills without them seeing us, we can make it through and out the other side and grab a car there."

"Okay."

Jackson knew she must be exhausted from the morning, but she gamely strapped her skis back on and ducked out behind the tree. "Lead on."

He grinned at her and dropped a swift kiss on her head. "You're a real trouper, Callie Martin. After me."

A small animal, startled by their sudden movement, crackled through the underbrush. The sound was like shotguns going off and Jackson knew they were in trouble. He paused to look long enough to see one man point toward them and another raise his rifle. "Duck, Callie."

The shot fell far short, but he knew they might not be so fortunate next time. Engines revved behind him. "Through the trees, Callie. We need to go some way they can't follow in the cars."

He was grateful for her athletic skills as they made a daring run through some pretty rough terrain straight into the heart of the woods. Jackson had no clue where they were, but he figured that was a good thing. If he didn't, hopefully the men after them didn't either.

After a half hour of straight-out skiing, Jackson called to her to stop. Callie gratefully drew to a halt.

"Are you okay?"

If she was honest, no. Her toes were numb, her face nearly frostbitten and her fingers totally cramped from her death grip on the ski poles. "Fine. Why did we stop?"

Jackson reached into his zippered pocket and pulled out his phone. "I need the GPS to tell me where we are."

He studied the coordinates while Callie drew in deep breaths and tried to knead some feeling back into her fingers.

"Looks like there's a small town over that ridge," Jackson said. "Do you think you can make it that far?"

She'd be going on sheer grit and determination, but there was no way she was giving up now. She nodded.

Another hour of icy torment brought them close to the

edges of the town. Dusk wasn't far off and Callie felt a
huge wave of relief at the sight of houses with lights. There
was a limit to how far even grit could take you."

Apparently cars could travel faster. "Jackson." Callie
wanted to cry. "Look."

Parked right in the middle of the main street was the
same black car they'd been warned about. If it hadn't been
distinguishable by how out of place it was, the men in black
parkas toting guns were a pretty good giveaway. She sank
to the ground before her legs could give out on her.

"Jackson, I want to keep going." She gasped, her breath
condensing in a cloud in front of her face. "But I don't
think I can. I don't want them to catch you because I can't
keep up."

Jackson crouched down beside her and took her face in
his hands. "Let's get one thing clear—I'm going nowhere
without you. Keeping you alive is my sole purpose in life
at the moment. I'm not abandoning you."

"But—"

"There are no buts." He cut her off with a quick kiss.
"Just sit here behind this garage while I look around." And
then he set off to assess the situation.

He'd kissed her. For the second time in less than twenty-
four hours, Jackson had shown feelings for her. But this
was different than last night's almost kiss. This had been
Jackson in a ferociously protective mode. Her lips tingled
in a way that had nothing to do with cold. It was more
like warmth flooding back into frozen fingers and toes.
It might hurt, but it was a sure sign of life. Jackson made
her feel alive in a way she never had before.

She waited for what felt like so long a time that she was
worried something had happened to him. When he finally
appeared around the side of the building, she couldn't contain the smile that burst across her face.

"I found us some transportation."

He stretched out a hand to help her up. Her cramped legs protested, but she stomped her feet a few times and got the feeling flowing again. What she wouldn't give for a warm fire and a hot drink.

"We have to walk through yards. But watch out at the fifth house. They let the dog out before so I had to circle around. That's what took so long." He dipped his head and smiled at her. "Sorry if you were worried."

They emerged at the end of the street and Callie's spirits took a nosedive. "A snowmobile?" Here she'd been envisioning heat and an interior.

"I'm sorry." Jackson rested his arm on her shoulders and gave her a hug. "I know you must be exhausted, but we have to get some distance between us and get to somewhere we can rent a car. I borrowed it from a really nice family."

She wanted to be positive, but the cumulative effect of everything was hitting hard right now. "Jackson, be honest. There's nothing we can do, is there? No matter where we go, somehow they find us."

"There has to be a reason why. Once I figure what that is, we'll be fine. For now, let's just get out of here before they start searching the town."

He handed her a pair of goggles and a helmet, and helped her onto the snowmobile. He donned his own gear, settled in front of her and told her to hold on tight. They started off slowly, heading up the back street to avoid detection. Jackson turned a corner and nearly swerved off the road when he saw the black car blocking the road. "Hang on, Callie."

He opened the throttle and they flew over the fields. Shots sounded behind them, and Callie clung tighter as he zigzagged down the road to make it harder to hit them. Hearing the car engine rev, Jackson took off across a rutted field.

Callie wondered if she hadn't been so exhausted, cold and scared of men shooting at her, if she might have enjoyed this ride. They followed a path into the woods and back out across a frozen river and over more snowy farmland. When they came to another lake, and it became clear Jackson wasn't going to stop, Callie squeezed her eyes shut and buried her head against his back.

Jackson laughed wildly. Clearly someone was enjoying this now that the enemy was left in the dust. "It's safe," he shouted and pointed to the huge sign indicating the ice was thick enough for vehicles. They hit the lake and flew ahead. He clearly knew what he was doing, and Callie had to admit it was an exhilarating experience to race across the frozen lake surface.

It was almost a letdown when they finally came to a town big enough to have a rental agency. They switched the snowmobile for a car and made arrangements to have the snowmobile returned to the family Jackson had borrowed it from.

"I wish I felt safe enough to rent a room and stay here the night."

"I know. We're not far enough away. It's okay. If you can stay awake to drive, I can deal with being a passenger."

Jackson grinned at her. "After that ride, I may never need to sleep again. The adrenaline rush is like an entire pot of caffeine."

His excitement was infectious. Callie smiled back. "I get it. Someday, when I'm not running for my life, I might actually like to try it again. But now," she pleaded. "Can we get some food and turn on the heat so I can thaw?"

Miles receded beneath the wheels as Jackson drove along the dark highway. Callie was asleep in the back and his heart had finally stopped feeling like it was pounding out of his chest. His brain was still racing as he mentally played out the various possible reasons why they could constantly be found. He'd checked Callie's phone and his own. They'd switched cars so many times that nothing could possibly be based on that. He was left with only unacceptable choices. Either Callie wasn't who she appeared to be, or someone within WITSEC couldn't be trusted.

He drove through the night, and dawn was edging the eastern sky when he felt his phone vibrating on the seat beside him. Given his train of thought, he was wary about answering. The display indicated it was his boss, so he had no choice but to pick up. Maybe there was news. "Sir?"

He knew the conversation would be tense when it opened with Mr. Logan demanding to know why he'd gone off radar.

"There's been some trouble," Jackson said.

"So I hear."

"I have the witness safe." Maybe that would be enough to placate the higher-ups.

"That's what matters."

Jackson drew a breath of relief. "How's Ben?"

After hearing that his mentor was on the road to recovery, Jackson glanced in his rearview mirror. Callie was still asleep, or pretending to be, so he asked the question that had been preying on his mind. "About what we discussed before." He waited until his boss asked if he meant about Callie being innocent. "Yes. Are you still certain?"

The silence that yawned over the phone was answer enough. "We're not sure. I had a long talk with DEA and the assistant US attorney. They're the reason the trial's been postponed. They want Callie. Want to find out what else she knows."

"I'm not bringing her in. Not until someone can unequivocally guarantee her safety. There have been at least four attempts to grab her. Three of them have happened within the past week. That tells me someone's running scared."

"Or she's involved."

No. Jackson thought of Callie enduring the incredibly hard conditions that they'd faced. No one would voluntarily go through that to escape unless it was life and death.

"It doesn't matter. Our deal is with her. Even if she's involved, she's small potatoes. We need the big guys, Jackson. You know that. Too many innocents have been hurt by these guys. If she was involved and gets away with it, it's a small price to pay for a bigger justice."

Jackson swallowed hard. The protein bar he'd snacked on felt lodged in his chest. This was the part of his job he really struggled with—letting lesser criminals go in order to catch the bigger ones.

"Jackson?"

"I hear you. So everything else is still in place?"

When he'd received an affirmative response, he disconnected the call.

He could hear Callie stirring in the back. Was she awake? How much had she heard? He kept his eyes on the road and said nothing. He wasn't ready to talk to her yet. He needed to get his thoughts clear.

And then there was the kiss. He'd almost kissed her on Christmas Eve, and he had kissed her last night. He couldn't stop thinking about those stolen moments. Kissing a witness he was protecting went against every instinctive sense of right and wrong for this job. He knew it was wrong. But he'd done it anyway.

It had felt so right. So…God-given.

Now where had that thought come from?

He shook it off as Callie's influence and forced his attention back to the news that his boss had delivered. The trial was definitely postponed, and they couldn't be sure Callie was innocent.

WITSEC would continue to protect her no matter what, but maybe Jackson needed to start protecting his heart.

TWELVE

Callie had awoken in the backseat to the sound of voices. One was loud. She recognized it as Jackson's. The muffled one, coming through the phone apparently, belonged to someone from his office. She couldn't make out the words from the other end, but it didn't take much to realize they were talking about her. Tension vibrated in Jackson's voice and it provoked a similar reaction in her, though it also saddened her. Something in the conversation, the tone more than the specific words, had conveyed a sense of disapproval.

Disappointment sank over her like a sodden blanket. After the near kiss she'd lain awake half the night, dreaming that possibly something was building between them. She was still processing last night's kiss, but she knew she'd fallen hard, and it was for all the right reasons. Jackson was a special man. Cute guys were a dime a dozen, but cute guys who were true gentleman and who would go out of their way for you were, in her experience, a rarity.

Jackson was all that and more.

But apparently he didn't feel the same way about her. She was his witness to protect—nothing more.

After he'd hung up the phone, Callie waited for him to say something. Did he think she was still sleeping? It didn't matter. If he'd had something to say, he would have said it. She tried to doze back into her dream world where they actually had a chance at a future together, but reality had closed that door.

"I know you're awake."

Callie pretended to yawn. So now he wanted to talk. "I am now. I've been dozing on and off. Your voice woke me earlier. Was that your boss?"

She felt his hesitation. "Yes. He had some information."

"And?" Maybe this would help explain his mood.

"There's a rest stop a mile up the road. Let's wait until we get there. I need coffee and I don't want to have this conversation while I'm driving."

That didn't bode well. Callie thought she might get sick.

Jackson pulled into the rest stop a few minutes later. "Do you want anything to eat?"

"No." She got out of the car and joined him in the front seat. "I just want to know why you're so upset." There. It was out there. Let him deal with it now.

"You were right," he said. "That was my boss on the phone."

Guilt swamped her. "How's Ben?" She'd barely even thought of him these past few days while she and Jackson were on the run.

"Recovering."

Callie offered a silent prayer. *Thank You, Lord. Ben was safe in Your hands even though I neglected to think of him.*

Callie's brow furrowed in confusion. "So what has you upset?"

"I'm not upset."

"Concerned, then. What has you so concerned that we had to pull over to talk?"

Jackson rested his head against the steering wheel. Fatigue seemed to weigh more heavily than usual and Callie's alarms sounded. "Jackson, what did he say?"

Jackson looked up and the sadness in his eyes spoke to her heart.

"They picked up the driver of the car. The one used in the kidnapping attempt in New York."

"Isn't that a good thing?"

"Yes. Of course. He talked. A little."

When he paused, she prompted, "And—"

"The men who grabbed Ms. Davis, the assistant US attorney, weren't intending to kill her."

"Oh, that's good." She smiled at him.

Jackson didn't return the smile. He sucked in his breath, then let it out slowly. "We were right that they really meant to take you."

"Oh." They'd been pretty sure that was the case, but in that instant Callie learned there was a world of difference between thinking it and having it confirmed. Her stomach felt suddenly hollow, and heat flashed through her body followed by chills that wracked her frame despite the heavy coat.

"There's more."

More. She didn't think she could take more. Enough. She raised one trembling hand to her lips while the other one grabbed for support, something to anchor her in a world that had tilted off axis yet again.

"He gave them a lead on one of the other kidnappers. DEA went to pick him up, but he was killed in the attempt."

Callie went pale. "That doesn't sound good."

"It's not. But once the driver heard about his partner's death, he found his voice and squealed like a stuck pig." Jackson paused, swallowed hard. "He told the feds the reason they were after you was not because of the men awaiting trial back in Texas."

"What?" Callie was totally confused. "Then why bother with me at all? I thought they wanted to protect their own men."

"The men are on their own. Big boss doesn't care about them. He wants you."

"How could that be? What does it mean?"

"That's what DEA is trying to figure out," Jackson responded.

"DEA. Like Drug Enforcement Administration? That was the other agent at the meeting? The one who saved the assistant US attorney."

Jackson nodded.

"He looked familiar. I think he was there the night Rick was killed. Part of the team of feds. At least I think it was him. DEA. Maybe. I really don't remember. It makes sense they would have been called in, though, right? Or was it FBI?" She gave a nervous laugh that held a tinge of bitterness. "Their jackets all look alike with those big letters." She had this vague memory of thinking she could play a kindergarten letter game with their jackets. "It sounds so much more serious with them involved."

"Callie." Jackson's voice was infused with frustration. "How much more serious does it have to get?"

"I know. That was a stupid remark." She buried her head in her hands. "I'm sorry," she mumbled through her fingers. "It doesn't really get much more serious than murder, does it?"

"It does when innocent people's lives are affected. That takes it to a whole new level."

Callie didn't want to lift her head. His voice had gotten so harsh. And she had the worst feeling that she wasn't the innocent person he was speaking of. Up until tonight, she'd felt they were on the same side. Suddenly she wasn't so sure.

As she sat there feeling sorry for herself, a new thought struck her. She sat back her seat, stunned. "That poor woman, the attorney. She had to go through that, an attempted kidnapping, just because she was working my case."

"It's one of the risks we take."

Callie fell silent. She sat there in stunned shock as she tried to process it all. This day just got worse and worse. Had it been only two days ago that she and Jackson had lazed on the sofa watching movies? Now he had nothing but curt replies. Despair pulled at her. He was her only hope. Her only connection to the world. She turned and stared at him, knowing all her desperation was probably showing in her eyes. She had no pride left, so what did it matter if she had to plead? "What am I supposed to do now?"

"What do you mean? Nothing's really changed. We keep you safe until you can testify."

Nothing had changed. Except his feelings about her. Except the tone of his voice. Except…whatever. Only one thing mattered now. "I have a condition," she told him, trying to sound firm. "I have to stay away from other people. I don't want anyone else hurt because they happen to be near me."

He appeared to think on it. "Agreed. As much as feasible."

Was it possible that his voice had softened just a bit?

He wasn't finished. "Before I make any promises, we have to figure out how they keep finding us. You're honestly not contacting anyone?"

The question perturbed her. "You're with me practically every waking moment. How would I be contacting anyone? More to the point, why would I want to?"

He didn't answer immediately, and his silence was a

light bulb moment for her. "Wait a minute." She swallowed hard, almost gasping for breath, struggling with the depth of his doubt. "You think I was in on it. You think I've been behind all of this.

"I thought." She swallowed again. Her mouth was so dry, she could barely breathe. There was no way she was going to tell him she'd thought they were building some kind of relationship. "I thought we were getting along well. But if…" She closed her eyes against the pain, fought for calm. "If you thought I was guilty…" Her voice died off as she thought of how he had kissed her before he went searching for the snowmobile. How kind he had been to her. All of that suddenly felt different. The kiss suddenly felt tawdry.

Why had he kissed her if he thought she was complicit in these crimes? Why had he gotten close to her at all? There were too many questions and she had no answers.

She was stuck with him. She had to rely on a man who didn't trust her to protect her. A part of her thought she might prefer to take her chances with the enemy. At least she always knew where she stood with them.

She turned and faced the side window as Jackson restarted the car and pulled back onto the highway. He hadn't gotten his coffee. The silly thought popped into her head, but she didn't have the strength to question him. Maybe his appetite had vanished like hers had.

Miles of yellow lines passed by in a continuous blur because of the tears in her eyes. Would she ever find anyone who truly cared for her?

Despair swamped her until finally she remembered to pray. Rote prayers at first because that's the way she had learned as a child to calm herself. She reminded herself that God loved her, and she prayed over and over until her breathing calmed and her anguish eased some. Little by little she tried to focus on her own words. *Dear Lord. You have a plan in this. Help me to accept Your ways even when I don't understand them.*

When she felt she had calmed enough, Callie broke the silence. "So how do I prove it's not me?"

She startled Jackson after being silent for so long. She sounded calm, in control. He guessed she'd been praying instead of crying as he'd assumed.

How did she prove it wasn't her? That was the question really. Was it true? Could she really not know anything, not be a part of it? Was it possible that she was as innocent as he wanted her to be?

The question hit like a punch to the gut, taking him down, hollowing him out. Jackson knew he had crossed some invisible line. Despite having good reason to suspect her, he was attracted to her and actually wishing they could pursue a relationship. Apart from the obvious problem of her heading into a new life with a new identity, she was his job, not his future.

He glanced at her but didn't say anything. He just waited. She finally continued. "You may think it's me, but it's not. I want to know what you're going to do to keep me safe. Whether you believe me or not, I want nothing more than to put these men away. Not just the men in jail. All of them."

She choked on the words for a minute. "They destroyed my life. Took everyone I loved from me, stole my dreams and killed my future. I have nothing to live for right now other than seeing them pay."

There was steel in her voice. It made her sound believable. That didn't necessarily make it the truth. The fact that he wanted so badly to believe her made him force himself to doubt.

"My job is to get you safely to trial. I will do that. You can take it from there." That was the best he could do. Keep it professional. "I'm tired. There's an airport in ten miles. Let's trade cars there, find someplace to stay and get breakfast. So long as neither of us alerted anyone, we should be good."

There was a bit of challenge in his voice but he didn't care. "Once we've eaten and I've slept, we can decide where to go from here."

Callie agreed, so he headed for the airport.

They hadn't gotten five of those ten miles when he caught sight of their tail. Pounding his fist against the wheel, Jackson stepped on the gas and took off down the highway.

"What's wrong?"

Her voice was less fearful and more resigned. As if she knew this was never going to end well.

"We seem to have found some friends again."

Callie didn't say a word. She averted her head as he glanced over but not before he saw the tear rolling down her cheek. With all they'd been through, he had yet to see her cry. Fighting back his own emotion, Jackson reached his hand toward her. She moved hers away.

Jackson blew out a breath. What had he expected after he'd confronted her with his suspicions? Better that he concentrate on evasion now anyway. This time he had no one to offer directions. He missed the spirit of camaraderie he and Callie had shared on the past few escapes. He might be the marshal, but they'd been operating as a team—and a good one. He'd have to think about that once they got out of this mess.

The other driver appeared to realize he'd been spotted and gave up any pretense of innocence, quickly closing the gap between them.

Looking around at the vast open spaces and light morning traffic, Jackson feared he was out of options. It was outrun them or...

An idea clicked. He had one major advantage now. The driver from New York had confirmed what had only been suspicion. These men were under orders to take Callie alive. Armed with that knowledge, it was an easy decision. Daring, but obvious. Where was the one place his pursuers wouldn't dare go?

Jackson gauged his time. His decision carried its own risks, but they were outweighed by the need to keep Callie safe. A gunshot aimed at his tire gave the final confirmation.

Tension clenched his jaw as the other car edged up on him, but he forced himself to be patient. He waited, counting down the mile markers, carefully calculating distance and speed, waiting until the car was almost upon him just as he came up to the airport sign. They were almost on his bumper when he stomped on the gas pedal and tore up the airport exit ramp.

The other driver followed, swinging wildly into the lane at the last minute. Side by side they sped along the service road.

"Callie? You okay?" Jackson didn't dare take his eyes from the road.

"I'm still alive."

"And I'm going to keep you that way. But hang on tight in five, four three, two, NOW." Jackson took a sharp right and blasted right through a security gate as the other car sailed on by. Sirens wailed as he slowed the car, gradually drawing to a halt. Within minutes the car was pulled over and surrounded, but Jackson smiled in satisfaction as he watched their tail speed away. This might require a pretty fancy explanation but at least they were safe for now.

He took his badge and held it out the window. "US Marshal. Don't shoot."

* * *

"That was awesome!"

Jackson chuckled at Callie's reaction. She was pretty awesome herself. Rather than terrifying her, his wacky plan seemed to have given her a punch of adrenaline. He grinned. "Just let me talk our way out of this, okay?"

It took several hours and many phone calls, but finally they were free to leave. Jackson wasn't sure if he'd end up with a promotion or a reprimand, but his witness was safe and in the end, that was all that mattered.

Jackson considered renting another car, but he was wary of heading back out on the road in case their tail was still waiting. Security had done a search, but he still didn't feel comfortable. The head of security came to his rescue, locating a couple of maintenance uniforms for them to borrow as a disguise.

They took a hotel shuttle out of the airport and within an hour they were in town and checked in at the hotel. Jackson declined a bellhop and escorted Callie to the assigned rooms.

She entered her room. He started to head to his own but stopped and walked back. Something was still bugging him. He knocked and called softly, "Callie, it's me."

When she opened the door, he pushed past her into the room. "This is crazy. Whatever may have happened before, I know you didn't call anyone and I know I didn't. There's got to be some kind of tracking device. I know you said Ben checked, and I've checked our phones, but we need to go through everything again. What do you have with you that you've had the whole time? Not anything you've bought since New York."

Callie closed the door and retrieved her bag from the desk. She dumped it on the bed. "I have this. Ben taught me to pack a small bag so I'd always have essentials no matter what. I had a Bible, too, but we left that at the cabin."

Jackson sifted through her things—toothbrush, toothpaste, hairbrush, aspirin, water bottle, wallet with her new ID, stuffed penguin. He picked up the stuffed penguin. "What's this? I haven't seen it before."

Callie blushed. "I know. I hid it because it looks silly for a grown woman to be carrying a stuffed animal in an emergency bag. It's from my class." She shrugged. "It helps me feel closer to home."

Jackson ran his fingers all over the plush animal, squeezing it. "Yeah, well it may be what is calling home, too. Feel this?" He guided her hands so she could feel the hard piece inside.

"I feel it. It's always been there. I figured it probably made some kind of sound, but it doesn't work anymore."

"Oh, it's making sounds all right, all the way to the people who are tracking us." He ripped open the seam and withdrew the tracking device.

"No," Callie protested, horrified at the implication. "That can't be. My students gave me this as a memento because we were doing a unit on penguins when I had to leave. They sent it to me so I wouldn't forget them."

"Who actually gave it to you? Think, Callie, it's important."

"I told you, my class." She looked near tears.

"No, I mean how did it get to you? You were in protective custody when you received it, weren't you?"

"Yes." She nodded. "Ben brought it to me. That afternoon, before the meeting. It was in a basket with some other things. He said my class parents put together a basket with presents. I knew I couldn't bring the whole thing, so I tucked this in my bag since it was pretty small." Her lips trembled. "I wanted something to remember my class, something that could still connect me to the life I knew. I'm sorry." Tears filled her eyes and spilled over. "I figured since Ben had given it to me it would be okay. I'm sorry."

Jackson paced across the room. He wanted to scream, to rant and rage. He wanted to roll back time, to never have gotten involved in this case. Ben had brought her the penguin with the tracking device. Ben, his friend, his mentor, his fellow marshal.

What did that mean? That Ben was a mole or just incredibly stupid? It was policy for marshals to sweep any gift for a tracking device. If he'd been doing his job properly, Ben couldn't have missed this. And what did it mean that Ben had been the one to escort the attorney down to the car—and the waiting kidnappers?

Jackson continued to pace, trying to figure out what to do next. On one of his turns, he looked up to see Callie standing by the window. She looked totally defeated. Jackson wanted to kick himself. He'd been so preoccupied with his own concerns about Ben and how ridiculous this whole situation was that he hadn't even stopped to think how it would affect her. Callie, who had been so resilient, so strong in the face of all adversity and determined even in the face of his doubt and disdain. This had crushed her.

He walked over and stood beside her. "Callie, honey, it'll be okay. Now we know. We can deal with this."

She looked up at him and he could see the tears still welling in her eyes.

"Someone in my class did this to me. A friend." Her voice changed cadence. "At least someone I considered a friend. Was it one of the parents? My student teacher?" She sucked in a breath. "I gave them everything. I thought we were like family."

He wrapped his arm around her shoulders, and when she rested her head against his chest, he pulled her into a hug. He stroked her hair, trying to comfort her. "It'll be okay, Callie."

She looked up at him and he thought he could drown in her sad eyes. "I'm the reason they've been following us everywhere. I could have gotten you killed."

He wanted to reassure her, promise her that no one from school had betrayed her, but he couldn't. He couldn't tell her he suspected Ben. He couldn't risk betraying a marshal if he was wrong. And he couldn't betray the marshal service if he was right.

"I'm sworn to protect you. I know the dangers. Think of it this way—at least now we know how they kept finding us."

She snuggled in deeper. He wanted to let her stay that way because he liked the feel of her in his arms far more than he should. "We'll figure it out. It isn't your fault. Ben should have known better than to give it to you without checking it." That was all he was going to say about it, but that alone spoke volumes. Ben did know better, which meant odds were it was intentional. A deep sadness stole over him, a feeling of betrayal that went deeper than the mere act. Ben had been his mentor, but more, he'd been his friend. Jackson couldn't even allow himself to think that his friend would betray him or a witness.

But if he didn't think it, he would possibly be putting that same witness in mortal danger. Already he'd endangered her by relying on Ben's check rather than doing his own.

"Callie." She shifted and when she looked up at him, her huge eyes still watery but calmer, he knew he would do anything to save her and it had nothing to do with the job. "We're going to have to leave. That thing's on," he gestured at the tracking device. "They'll be after us in no time."

"But if we leave it here, and they find it, they'll know we know."

"Exactly. So we need a plan." He walked over to the window and stood staring at the passing traffic as he thought it through. He didn't want to lose the tracking device. It was potential evidence. But they obviously couldn't keep it. He needed an answer fast.

A sound diverted his attention and he looked up in time to see a plane fly overhead. The hotel must be in the flight path. He could see another taking off in the distance.

A grin stole across his face as he turned to face Callie. "I know what to do." He strode across the bed to the mangled penguin. "Do you want me to save the stuffed-animal part?"

She shuddered. "No. That will never bring me anything but sad memories now. Do whatever you want with it."

He silently vowed to make it up to her somehow. While he was stuffing the device back into the penguin he gave her something to distract her attention. "Check to see if there's a binder in the desk. You know, the thing they usually have with all the local information."

She went to the desk and flipped through the pages. "Got it."

"Is there a phone number for the airport?"

"What?"

"Our little friend is going on a trip. Let's see… Where should we send him?"

Callie looked confused, but she picked up on his mood and tried to get in the spirit of things. "My class gave him to me because I love to sing. Don't you think a penguin should be on Broadway?"

He laughed out loud—a really happy sound after the day they'd had.

"New York it is! Though he may have to settle for starting Off-Broadway."

"Jackson, I really have no clue what you're talking about. We're going to put the penguin on a plane? Do we have to buy him a ticket?"

Jackson laughed. "No, we're going to ask for a little help from our new friends at the airport." She still looked confused, so he continued. "If we keep it with us, they'll just keep following. If we ditch it here, they'll know we know and they'll be looking for another way to find us. But if it looks like we're moving, they'll follow in the wrong direction. That will buy us time to get away."

She took a moment to process his logic. "Okay. But there's one thing." She seemed nervous. "If we send this off with someone else, will we be putting them in danger?"

His smile eased as he considered her question. He didn't allow himself to dwell on the way his heart expanded at her show of concern for others at a time when she was in danger. "No. It will be okay. They never do anything until they actually see you. If they don't see you, if you're not there, it won't be a danger to anyone else."

She looked reluctant. "If you're sure."

He wasn't sure about anything except the need to get away. "We need to get going. They're probably on the way here right now. Grab the rest of your stuff." He opened the door a crack and looked out while she hastily repacked her bag. "All clear. Ready?"

"Yes."

They headed to the elevator, but as they stood waiting, the floor lights showed an elevator coming up. Their eyes met.

"We're not taking any chances. Come on."

THIRTEEN

Jackson grabbed her hand and made a dash for the stairway. They ran down a few flights. When Jackson tried the reentry door it was locked. Suddenly they heard voices on the stairs above them.

"I think they found us," Callie whispered.

"Shh. They won't be sure if they don't hear us."

Footsteps rang out on the steps above. Callie looked at Jackson and mouthed, "Really?"

They took off down the stairs again. Just three more flights and they'd be at street level.

A gunshot echoed in the stairwell. The bullet slammed into the wall, too close to Callie's head for comfort. Jackson reacted instinctively and covered her. He kept her protected by the bulk of his body as they raced down.

With one flight to go to the street, another bullet whizzed by as they reached the lobby-level door. Jackson tried the door and breathed a ragged sigh of relief to find it unlocked. But the space they exited into was big and open. They'd be sitting ducks the minute their pursuers cleared the door.

Out of the corner of his eye, Jackson spied the fire-alarm bell. "Come on." He pulled Callie and reached for the alarm.

He offered a mental apology to the firemen for what was about to happen. Callie stared at him in disbelief as she watched him break the glass and pull the lever. "This definitely qualifies as an emergency. Hopefully it will slow them down and we can get lost in the crowd."

He didn't wait for her to agree. The alarm rang out, its shrill sound echoing throughout the hotel. There was mass confusion as people came running from every direction. Jackson dragged Callie along, letting them get swept up in the forward rush. He could hear the yelling behind them, but they were soon swallowed up by the crowd.

Jackson guided Callie around the corner. Everyone else was gathering across the street, but he headed directly toward an office building on the next block. He pulled her to safety in the lobby. A flash of his badge got them through security. Jackson stopped long enough to tell the officer on duty that he was protecting a government witness, and if anyone tried to come in after them, to please detain them.

They rode the escalator to a first-level lobby, where a crowd of workers had gathered to watch what was going on across the street. Jackson guided Callie to a corner where they could stand behind some plants and look out. He stood closely behind her.

"There. See them?" Jackson pointed to a few men looking wildly around. One was checking some sort of GPS device. He suddenly turned and pointed at the building they were in.

Callie looked over her shoulder at Jackson with an expression every bit as disgusted as he felt.

"There's a plus side," he told her. "We have visual confirmation that's how they were tracking us."

"That's comforting."

"Security will keep them for a bit."

"You think?" Callie gave a look at their maintenance getup. "Are you sure he believed you?"

"He will when they try to come through and he sees I was right. Come on. We'll take the back escalator down and grab a cab to the airport."

Airport security didn't appear exactly thrilled to see them again, but once Jackson explained the situation, the officer agreed to supply packing materials and get the dangerous toy on the next flight back to Texas.

Jackson addressed the package to headquarters back in San Antonio. "Sorry, fella. No Broadway for you." Jackson hoped he would have the last laugh because if the men followed it, he'd be sending them right to the marshals' office.

But he wasn't in a laughing mood. That penguin was headed back to the very same marshals' office that likely harbored a traitor. A very sober Jackson handed over the package.

Jackson's mood didn't improve even after they were back on the road. Callie waited for him to say something, but he was unusually quiet. Despite their apparent truce, he held himself aloof.

His mistrust weighed heavily on her. She cared about him. It mattered that he didn't believe her. Finally she couldn't take it anymore. Her voice pierced the stillness. "Do you believe yet that I'm innocent?"

Jackson glanced over at her from the driver's seat. "It's my job to be suspicious."

"That's a cop-out."

He seemed stunned that she called him on it. "Why do you say that?"

"Because you can still protect me without doubting me. I've given you no reason to think I'm anything other than who I say I am and no reason to believe I was ever any more involved than I said I was."

Except that she had hidden the penguin from him. Until he could talk to Ben, he had only her word on things. "Do we have to have this discussion while we're driving?"

"Apparently so. We can't let it continue to stand between us. Or someone probably will get hurt because we're acting like enemies, not partners."

"We're not partners, Callie. It's my job to protect you. I'm the marshal and you're the witness. Not partners."

She muttered under her breath.

"What was that?"

"Never mind. Jackson, talk to me, please. I don't understand how you can go from giving me my best Christmas ever to acting like I'm a piece of drug-dealing trash."

"I never said any such thing," Jackson protested. "But the evidence has been stacked against you from the start."

That was news to Callie. "How so?"

"I can't believe we're having this conversation."

"Well, we are. So let's hear it."

"When did you get so tough?"

Tough? She felt like her life was falling to pieces around her. She wasn't tough. Just desperate. "Please, Jackson. I need to understand. Why would anyone think I was involved?"

He lifted one hand off the wheel to rub it over his eyes and forehead. "Okay. First the killings. You were the only one who got away alive."

Callie gasped. The pain that he would even suggest…

He darted a look at her. "You asked. I'm not going to gloss over it. Do you want to hear the answer or not?"

She swallowed her tears and nodded. "Yes," she murmured, realizing he couldn't see her head motion.

"Then there was the meeting. You denied knowing anything about the case, but you stayed upstairs while an attack was made on the assistant US attorney."

"Ben told me to stay up there. I was upset."

He glanced over and raised an eyebrow. "That does not help your case. Neither does it help that once we were on the run, there was attempt after attempt where they just missed us—but they always knew exactly where we were."

"You already know the reason for that. The tracking device that I did not put in the penguin."

"I haven't been able to reach Ben to confirm that yet. Be reasonable. You hid it from me. If you try to put yourself in my shoes, can't you understand even a little why I might doubt you?"

She tried to think of it from his point of view. Finally she shook her head. "No."

"No?"

"Ben had given it to me, so I didn't think there was any need to show you. And I can't put myself in your shoes and see how you see it because I know I had nothing to do with it. Remember how I broke down, told you he left me with nothing? Well it's worse than that. I have less than nothing now because I don't even have hope for the future."

Callie knew she was laying her emotions bare, but what did it matter? She had absolutely nothing left to lose. "I felt like you and I had connected. I felt like you cared about me." She couldn't quite bring herself to say *for* me. "But that's all a fraud if you can't even take my word as truth."

Jackson didn't respond. Because she was making an impression? She kept on, trying to make him see. "I can't even imagine why you would think I would be involved. My ex-boyfriend was killed."

She hesitated for a moment. How honest should she be? She hated to lay bare any more, but what was one more layer of skin when she'd already opened herself so much?

"Maybe he wasn't the love of my life. Maybe we didn't have a future together, but he was a good person. I do believe that. He was someone I cared about.

"Maybe…okay, definitely, he made some bad choices, but now I'll never get to ask him why. I could be the kind of cold, judgmental person who writes him off because he got involved with drug dealers—and trust me, in my brain, I've done that a few times. I did break up with him. But the Gospel teaches us about forgiveness. And justice. I want justice for him. I have to forgive him in my heart because he's not here anymore, so there's no point in holding on to a grudge I'll never understand."

The atmosphere in the car thawed ever so slightly. She got the sense that maybe Jackson was listening with his heart rather than his badge. "I need justice for him. I will testify so the men who ruined my life won't have that chance to ruin someone else's. I—" She fell quiet. Maybe she'd said too much already.

"What aren't you saying?" Jackson prompted.

Callie looked at him. He was driving slowly, as if to be sure his concentration was on her. "What do you mean?"

"At the end. You were thinking something else you didn't say."

"How can you know me that well and still not know that I'm telling the truth?" She didn't wait for an answer. "I was thinking that once upon a time I'd hoped to have a future with him."

"But the killers destroyed that." Jackson finished for her.

"No. He did."

Silence stretched out until eventually she spoke softly. "All I wanted was a home, a family, people to love. He wanted something different, the big things. Fancy car, monstrosity of a house, money to travel, money to entertain, money to do things big."

"And you didn't want that."

"I didn't want any of that. I just wanted us to be a family. But I guess that wasn't enough for him since apparently he was dealing drugs to make that money." Her voice trailed off. "But that was him, not me." She whispered the last words as if her defense had depleted all her energy. "His mistake. Not mine. But it became my burden."

FOURTEEN

Jackson heard the broken *I wasn't enough* that she didn't voice, and his heart ached for her. Maybe because he understood that kind of loneliness.

His own heart had been hurting all afternoon. There could be no romantic resolution for them, but at least he could try to calm things between them so they could part on better terms. And have good memories to hang on to for the inevitable lonely nights.

His voice was soft when he began to speak. His peace offering came from deep within him, and his tone echoed the reticence of sharing something long held private.

"Years ago, there were some other men who wanted money for big things. They didn't care how they got it either. Didn't care who they hurt. They broke into my parents' home."

His mouth had gone dry so he stopped long enough to take a swig from his water bottle. "No one was expected to be home, but plans had changed and my whole family was there—except for me. My parents and my brother, Sam, were there."

His voice cracked on Sam's name. "The thieves got scared and started shooting. It was a massacre."

Callie's soft gasp reached right into his soul. "Jackson, I'm so sorry."

He couldn't acknowledge her sympathy. If he did, he'd

never finish. "Everyone in the neighborhood knew who had done it, but they were terrified. No one would testify against the murderers."

"Don't tell me they got off."

"Scot-free. Not a day spent in jail because there was no evidence against them. As a teen, I was pretty sure even the police were scared of the connections, though no one ever admitted it.

"I made a vow that day that I would fight for justice for other families." He paused, swallowed hard. "So yes, I understand when you say you intend to testify so others won't have to face this."

Callie didn't respond immediately. He could see from her expression that she was processing everything he'd said. Her expression seemed to soften. "I guess that makes it a little easier to accept your reasons for doubting me." She reached over and rested her head on his shoulder. "You don't need to. We're on the same side here, Jackson."

He glanced down at her and smiled sadly. "I guess we are. Now we just have to find a way to make sure we're the winning side."

"We can," she vowed. "If we do it together. If we work as partners."

Jackson looked at the lovely, brave girl beside him. Even when he'd doubted her he'd acknowledged her courage. He only wished they could be more than partners, could build something together.

"So now where do we go?"

Jackson laughed. Here he was being all sentimental and she was all business. "Where would you like to go? Dream big."

"A horse farm in Kentucky."

Jackson blinked. "That's big. Where did that idea come from?"

Callie sighed wistfully. "I told you I loved horses. As a little girl, I used to dream of living on a ranch or on a farm, raising race horses." She shrugged. "You told me to dream big. I've never told anyone before. But you asked."

So he had. The implication being that no one else ever had. No one had cared enough what she wanted. He'd file that information away for later. "How about for tonight we just find a small city with a nice hotel?"

"Sounds good. I'm suddenly starving."

They had three days to rest up. On the fourth day, just when they were getting restless, Jackson got a phone call. When he hung up, he stood staring into space, trying to figure out what could possibly be going on.

Callie obviously knew his expressions well by now. She took one look at his face and said, "What's wrong?"

He drew in a long breath and exhaled very slowly. "I don't know quite how to tell you."

"Just spill it. The tension only makes it worse."

He knew what she meant. No amount of waiting was going to make this news any easier to deliver or bear. "The men you were supposed to testify against…" He paused, closed his eyes a second. "They were killed in a prison fight."

Her gasp cut right to his heart. She sank down on the sofa, shock written across her face as she tried to grapple with the news.

"An accident?"

"Not likely."

A look of terror crossed her face at those two words. He knew what she must be thinking. If the men were expendable, what about her?

"So, what do we do now? I seem to always be asking you that question, but honestly what happens now? My whole point of existence these past months has been to stay alive to testify against the men who killed Rick and his friends. To find justice."

She visibly crumpled as the full impact hit her. She leaned forward, elbows on her knees, her hands cradling her face as if the weight of it all was too much for her neck to bear. "Now I won't get that chance."

She sat like that for so long that Jackson assumed she was praying and gave her time. Finally she lifted her gaze. "What did they tell us to do? Do I even need to stay in witness protection anymore if I don't get to testify?"

"This just happened, so they're not sure yet what's next. I guess yes, they think there's reason for you to stay in. I promise, Callie, when I know more, you will. For now we're supposed to stay deep under until they figure out what's up."

"Because we've had such success with that so far."

"Remember, we don't have the tracking device anymore. No one tracked us here. Anyway, there's a farmhouse a couple hours' drive from here—it's a safe house. We're supposed to hole up there."

"Do they have any idea who killed them? Was it their own people or other inmates who knew what they'd done?"

"It's too soon to tell."

"But they think it was their own, don't they?" Callie twisted her fingers, rubbing them back and forth before knotting her hands into fists.

Jackson nodded slowly. "Most likely. No offense to your boyfriend, but he wasn't the type of victim who would arouse animosity inside. That's saved for certain types of offenders."

"How soon do we leave?"

She took one look at his face and wearily lifted herself off the sofa. "I'll get my bags."

FIFTEEN

Callie was bored. She didn't want to complain, but endless days of reading and watching television were driving her mad. "Is this what your work is always like?"

Jackson looked up from the wooden horse he was carving. "Pretty much."

"Aren't you bored to tears?"

"You mean when I'm not getting shot at or racing snowmobiles across frozen lakes or running down stairwells or—"

Callie laughed. "Okay, I get it. But seriously, how do you deal with the mind-numbing tedium of being cooped up with a witness for days on end?"

He smirked at her. "Tedium? Aren't we into fancy words?" He rose, set his tools aside and stretched, trying to unkink his knotted shoulder muscles.

She laughed again. "Come on, you have to know what I mean."

"I do. I just like the sound of your laugh." He surrendered with a wink. "It's part of the job and honestly…" He shrugged and gave her a sheepish grin. "I kind of prefer this to the hail of bullets. Hope that doesn't ruin your impression of me."

Callie got into the spirit and played along. "Oh, no! My

heroic marshal is a coward. He runs from trouble rather than toward it."

He raised an eyebrow. "I prefer to think of that as highly intelligent rather than cowardly. How about, your marshal uses his brilliantly developed mind to escape nefarious criminals and protect innocent victims?"

"My hero!" Callie gushed.

"Now that's more like it. Go ahead and swoon."

Callie stood and pretended to faint. Jackson jumped to catch her as she fell. She was laughing as she landed in his arms, but her sense of humor faltered as she glanced up into his eyes. Eyes that were suddenly much too close to hers. She tore her gaze away, but it settled on lips that were also too close to hers. Firm lips, kissable lips, lips that opened as he breathed and softly sighed. Lips that were on hers, touching hers.

Jackson shifted and lost his balance. They were laughing again as they landed on the sofa, but laughter stilled as he recaptured her lips. He pulled her into his arms and settled more comfortably beside her on the couch.

"This could become my favorite way of passing the time," he whispered when he finally drew back. He grinned at her and she took a playful swat at him.

"I'm sure you say that to all your witnesses."

He sobered up then, her words rushing over him like an icy waterfall. "No. And I shouldn't have allowed it with you, but…"

She silenced him with another quick kiss. "You don't want your witness to be bored, right? She might do something foolish."

"What could be more foolish than us falling for each other?" Jackson pulled back, tried to be disciplined. His phone rang. "Saved by the bell," he joked as he reached for it and glanced at the display. "Walker here."

Callie rose and wandered over to the window. The fire was crackling, making the room warm and cozy. Light snow was falling outside. Her lips tingled from the memory of Jackson's kiss.

Callie glanced at him reflected in the glass as he chatted on his phone. All serious, there was no sign of the playful man who had kissed and cuddled with her mere moments earlier.

What had she been thinking? As he'd said, it was foolish. There was no future for them, no way they could ever be more than client and marshal. He had a career protecting witnesses. She was headed into a new identity with witness protection, provided they still thought she needed to be in the program. Once the DEA figured out what was happening, she'd be packed off to wherever and never see him again.

That thought chilled her in a way no fire could warm. It didn't change how she felt about him, though. Wasn't it just the story of her life? She seemed destined never to have anyone to love.

Why, Lord? Do You want me to be alone? Is there some higher purpose to me never having someone to love? I'm trying to see Your will, but honestly all I see is how lonely I feel. I'm trying, Lord. I'm thankful that You put Jackson in my life to keep me safe from harm, but who is going to keep my heart safe from him? I'm coming to care for him far more than is good. How can that be Your plan?

She stared out the window in silence for a few minutes. The prayer changed as her heart surrendered. *I know You know all, Lord. Please help me to trust in You, to trust that You have a plan for me. I will trust in You, oh Lord, my God.*

Jackson was a good man. She thanked the Lord for letting her get to know him. She wasn't really sorry for wishing she could know him a little bit better. For just a few minutes she let herself daydream about how life could be if she weren't in witness protection. Imagine if she could embrace a future with him. Imagine if she could fall in love, marry and have lots of little Jacksons.

Callie was still dreaming of playing with toddlers on the floor when she realized Jackson had hung up the phone. He didn't say anything, but she knew from the look on his face that something was wrong.

She fought for composure. *Your will, not mine, oh Lord.* "What happened?"

"You'd better come sit down," Jackson replied.

"You know, I always hate when they say that on television. I hate it even more in real life. Please just tell me what happened."

"Someone broke into your apartment."

"Okay." She swallowed uneasily. That was not good, but she couldn't return there anyway, so what difference did it really make?

"They didn't just break in. They trashed the place—obviously looking for someone or something."

That sounded more serious. "What were they looking for? Do we know if they found it?"

"Presumably they did not."

His tone sounded ominous. "What makes you say that?" Callie braced herself.

"They also searched—trashed—your classroom."

"Oh, no!" This was a completely different situation than having her empty apartment trashed. "My babies! Was anyone hurt?"

Jackson shook his head. "No one was in the building at the time. Apparently it happened overnight. The maintenance staff discovered it when they went to unlock the rooms this morning."

She was silent for a few minutes, taking it all in. "Jackson, what does this mean?"

"Aside from the fact that they're looking for something?"

"Or someone. Could they still be looking for me?"

"They could. Probably are. But the way the apartment was trashed suggests they were looking for something, not someone. I'm guessing once they realized they'd lost track of you, they needed another way to find whatever it is they're looking for."

"Which is?"

Jackson sighed. "We were hoping you might have some clues about that."

That again. "I don't. How many times, how many ways do I have to say that I have nothing, no idea if Rick was hiding something? What kinds of things could they be looking for? I don't think he was hiding drugs there. I don't think he would have done that to me. I don't think he would have betrayed me like that."

Callie sank down onto a chair. "I do think he loved me in his own way, and I don't think he would risk endangering me or my children. He cared about them, too. He used to come and do sing-alongs in the classroom. He loved spending time with them before he got involved with bad things. He would never have put them in danger willingly." She buried her face in her hands. "At least I don't think he would. What do I know?"

"Why don't we go for a walk and let the cold air clear our heads? Maybe we'll figure something out."

"I don't think so. It's freezing." She shivered, wanting nothing more than to curl up in a ball before a warm fire.

Jackson knelt to stir the embers and rebuild the fire. Callie stared at his wide shoulders and couldn't help but think of the burden he always bore. She didn't want to increase it. Truth be told, she wanted to be the one to lighten it.

"I'll stop being such a wimp and brew us a pot of coffee," Callie offered. "Maybe caffeine can help us figure out what's going on."

The sound of an approaching car caught Callie's attention as she filled the coffeepot with water. She walked back into the living room and peered out behind the edge of the heavy curtain. "Jackson, there's someone coming to the door."

Jackson was instantly on alert and came to look over her shoulder. "Go into the bedroom and hide in the closet," he whispered. "I'll see what's up. It might be completely innocent." He didn't believe that for a minute.

Rather than open up the house to a stranger, Jackson donned his heavy coat and boots, and slipped out the back door. He grabbed a shovel off the deck and circled the house, coming up behind the man on the porch. "Afternoon. Can I help you with something?"

The man swiveled, and the look of shock on his face confirmed to Jackson that he was no innocent visitor. Jackson leaned against the porch railing, his hand on the shovel handle, ready to use it if necessary.

The stranger stepped back down the stoop. "Name's Wilson. I live down the road. Saw smoke from the chimney and wondered if someone had moved in. Neighbors have to stick together out here."

Jackson nodded. He had to play this carefully, not seem unduly concerned by a visitor. "Right neighborly of you. I'd invite you in to get acquainted, but my sister is taking a nap. She hasn't been well. That's why Thomas let us stay here. I don't want to disturb her."

"No problem," the man replied. "Just wanted to welcome you to the neighborhood, so to speak. We'll have plenty of time to visit when the weather eases. Hope you have wood stacked in—there's a storm brewing."

"Really?" Jackson feigned ignorance, though he had seen it on his weather app a short time ago. "Thanks for checking in on us. I'm sure we'll be fine. We stopped at the store and stocked up to stay for a while."

"You can find me a few miles down the road if you need anything."

"Thanks," Jackson offered his gloved hand, and the man shook it before heading back to his car.

Jackson stood on the porch, watching the taillights disappear in the gathering gloom. The visitor left him feeling uneasy, but the forecast was bad and he didn't want to head out into weather that would be more dangerous than staying put. Was he being overly suspicious? Was it possible the man was exactly who he said he was?

Possibly, but coupled with the news of Callie's apartment and school being searched, instinct said to be wary. He didn't want to alarm Callie, but he'd keep watch and as soon as the storm was past, they'd be moving again.

As it turned out, they didn't have that long. He'd only been on watch a few hours when they came.

"Callie," Jackson whispered in her ear. "Wake up. There's someone outside."

She came awake with a jerk. "What?"

"Shh. I've been worried ever since the so-called neighbor stopped by, so I was keeping watch. I don't think he was your average neighbor. They don't usually come calling at four a.m. with a couple of friends and shotguns."

She was wide-awake now. "What do we need to do?"

This was one of the things he loved about her. No complaints. Just a request for directions. "I'm going to go check on them again. I wanted you to have time to get your stuff together. Dress warmly. Layer up. I don't know how long we'll be outside, and the storm is bearing down."

The weather troubled him. Abandoning a warm shelter for unknown dangers in a storm seemed anything but wise under ordinary circumstances, but the men outside made the wild weather seem like a safer choice.

Once Callie was ready, she came to the bedroom door. "What are you planning?"

Jackson looked thoughtful. "There's a part of me that would like to sneak out and make a huge display and distract them so that you can make a run for it."

"No! I'm not going anywhere without you."

"Agreed." He was relieved to hear her say that. He'd needed to check. "Given the weather, I really don't think we should separate. Since it's the middle of the night, our best chance is to sneak out the back while they think we're still sleeping."

"Do you think they plan on attacking while we're sleeping?"

"Probably or they would have just attacked when our neighbor came by earlier. I told him we'd be staying awhile, so I imagine they feel there's no rush. Except to retrieve whatever their boss wants—which I'm guessing is you."

Callie grimaced.

"Look, can we discuss it later? Right now we should concentrate on getting away before they realize we're awake."

He was right. "What do I do?"

"Come here." He pulled her in front of him at the side of the window. "See that bunch of trees over there?"

He could feel her response as she breathed in. "Yes."

"There are two men in the midst of the trees. They haven't moved in an hour."

"What do you think they're waiting for?"

Much as he hated to admit it, Jackson had no idea. He shrugged as he backed away. "Maybe someone else is coming. Could be they're just keeping watch."

"Are you sure there's no one else?"

"I've checked from every window, and I don't see anyone. Do you want to look?"

"Okay. I trust you, but another pair of eyes can't hurt." Before she turned away, she noticed a movement. "Jackson," she whispered. "One of them changed position."

He came back to stand beside her and immediately saw that one of the two had walked around to the side.

"If it's only two of them, would we be better off capturing them as they come in?" Callie asked.

Jackson chewed on his lip as he mulled it over. He was pretty impressed by her bravery and can-do attitude. "We could. But what if they're waiting for someone? If more of them come, it will be too late to change our plans."

Almost as if his words had conjured it, she heard the muffled noise of a snowmobile coming down the road.

Jackson made a quick decision. He grabbed his huge duffel bag. "Let's get ready and head out the back while they're distracted by the new guy's arrival."

"Okay, but how do we get out?"

"There's a sliding glass door on the deck that leads to a hot tub. How are your climbing skills?"

She grinned. "I guess we'll find out."

Resisting the urge to take another glance out the window, Jackson led her into the master bedroom. As they slipped out onto the deck, he heard the low rumble of yet another snowmobile. Time to move it.

Fortunately, there was no sign of anyone in the trees on this side of the house. Keeping to the shadows, away from the outside spotlights, they stealthily made their way across the deck, climbed over the railing, dropped their bags to the ground and gently eased down into the snow. Once Callie was on the ground, he followed.

He gestured to the pine trees, then whispered in her ear. "I know it will be cold, but I think we should slither on our bellies so as not to attract attention. Hopefully it won't look as obvious as footprints."

Once again Callie was grateful for the one-piece snow-suit he'd bought her. At least snow was only trickling in a few places. As soon as they hit the tree line, they knelt, then eased up to stand behind two trees. Jackson, wearing the duffel like a backpack, held up a hand, signaling to her to wait a few moments to be sure no one had noticed them.

He pointed his finger and they made their way from one tree to another deeper into the woods and down to the shoreline. Fortunately, the snowy sky lent a brightness to the night, helping them see their way. Once Jackson figured they were far enough away, they paused to catch their breath and reassess.

The snow was light now, but Jackson wasn't planning on being fooled. "I saw the weather report. We have to find someplace to take shelter before it gets bad."

"What if we hide out here for a while and then go back to the safe house once they've discovered we're gone? At least we'd have somewhere warm to stay."

"It's tempting," Jackson admitted. "But I think it's too dangerous since we don't know where they're staying. Or whether they'll leave. Based on how things have been going, they'll probably decide to wait out the storm in our house and we'll be stuck out in the blizzard."

Callie slumped against a tree. "You've got a look in your eye. What are you thinking?"

Jackson smiled at her and chuckled softly. "I don't have

survivalist training for nothing. You're going to learn to build a tree-pit shelter."

Callie stared at him for a long moment. How much more ridiculous could this situation get? Realizing he was serious, she shrugged. "Sure. Why not?"

Jackson unpacked a folding shovel from his backpack. "First I have to choose a tree."

Callie laughed softly. "This feels like Christmas again."

He appreciated how she kept her sense of humor. "We need bushy branches for overhead cover. Can you find some of them while I dig the hole? Don't go farther than I can see."

By the time Callie had finished gathering pine boughs, Jackson had dug a sizable hole around the base of the tree.

"Now what?" she asked.

"Did you notice if they had dogs?"

Callie considered it. "I didn't see any, and I certainly didn't hear any."

"Good. The only way this structure will fail us is if dogs sniff us out." Jackson continued to dig and then pack the snow around the top and inside to create a solid wall. "Help me spread the branches on the ground for cover. We'll pull the rest over us once we settle in."

Callie did as he asked, handing the branches down to him. She unrolled the sleeping bags from his duffel and dropped them down, too. "It's going to be rather cozy in there, isn't it?"

He grinned at her. "Afraid?"

"Hmm. I have to choose between tight quarters with my handsome marshal or the men who want me either dead or alive. Tough choice."

Jackson decided to ignore the comment for now, lest his overheated reaction melt their shelter. "Throw our knapsacks down to me, then jump in." He extended a hand to help her. "I'll cover us up.

Callie laughed when they were settled in. "I feel like we're sitting inside a pot."

Their shelter did bear a resemblance to a pressure cooker, Jackson decided. In more ways than one.

"At least we're safe from the storm and the men."

Their gazes caught and lingered, and he knew they were sharing the same thought. Were they safe from each other?

SIXTEEN

"Jackson, since we're stuck in here with no place to go, can I ask you a question?"

He nodded.

"What's witness protection really like in the long haul?"

He chewed on his lip, trying to decide how to answer. "I can't deny it'll be tough and lonely at first. Until you can make friends. But you're always going to hold yourself a bit aloof."

"I'm used to holding back, but...do any of your witnesses ever marry?"

Jackson struggled not to let his shock show. There was no place here for his personal reactions. "Why do you ask that?"

"I'm just wondering if that means I'll never have the chance. I mean, what kind of trusting relationship can you build on a lie like that about your own identity?"

Jackson wished he could reassure her. Wished he could tell her it would all work out, but there was a good likelihood it wouldn't.

He needed to be honest. "I wish I could say yes. But I don't know of any cases offhand. Of course once people are off our radar, we don't necessarily know what they decide to do, so I can't say never."

They sat in companionable silence, each lost in their own thoughts.

Jackson broke the silence. "One of the things I've come to admire about you is your strong faith. That will get you through this. I know it."

Callie thanked him.

"I keep saying I'm going to ask you about it. We've got nothing but time now. Can you share your story with me?"

Callie hesitated. "I've never been the kind of person who went out and talked about God all the time. My relationship with Him always felt too personal."

Jackson looked around the tight quarters only dimly illuminated by a covered flashlight. "Only me here, Cal. I'd really like to listen. I shouldn't say this because it's not about our relationship, but you've changed me. You've opened up my perspective on a whole host of things."

He shifted to move a twisted pine branch. "Your faith has gotten you through some really tough times. I'd like to learn to believe, to trust like that."

Callie's response was self-deprecating. "My path isn't exactly noble or particularly inspiring."

He stared at her.

"Okay. But don't say I didn't warn you. You know I had a pretty scattered life, moving from home to home. Finally, I met a friend at school who started asking me to come to her church. I did—just really so I could have someone to go to brunch with afterward."

Jackson laughed softly. "The not-so-noble part?"

She smiled. "I know. It sounds terrible. But I was so desperately in need of family, and this church made me feel like I had one. The brunch was like the kind of Sunday meal other families shared.

"Anyway, that church was really big on community and fellowship. I started to learn more about how God wants us to be responsible for each other. Jesus's commandment to love one another, to love our neighbor hit home with me, so I started getting more involved and the more I got involved, the better I felt about my life, my relationship with God, my friends."

Pausing, she shifted to pull the sleeping bag a little higher. "I guess I should have realized when Rick wasn't interested in being with my church family that something was wrong. He told me he believed, but he was always working or making excuses for why he couldn't be with me at church or at any of our activities."

She stopped and shook herself. "I'm sorry. I didn't mean to go off like that. I don't know—"

"Don't apologize." He reached out to grasp her hand. "He messed with your life. I get that it matters." He squeezed her fingers in a gentle show of support. "Keep talking. Other than the chaplain, no one has ever really talked to me about their faith before."

"Really? It doesn't feel like I'm preaching at you?"

Jackson shook his head. "Not at all."

"I've always felt like I could be a better testament to the Lord's love through my actions. Words feel preachy."

"Your words don't. They help me to understand you."

"I read something once that said we should try to live each day so that others see Jesus in us. I'm probably not a very good model of that, but I do try to live my life with that goal."

Jackson realized he was still holding her hand. He laced his fingers through hers. "You've been that to me. I've learned more about Jesus and faith from you in the last week than I did in the whole of my previous life. You live your faith. That's inspiring." And so very attractive, but he didn't think he had any right admitting that out loud.

They sat in companionable silence for a while. Callie was stifling yawns and he was feeling pretty drowsy himself, but him sleeping wasn't wise under the current conditions. No reason Callie had to stay awake, though.

"I woke you from a sound sleep. Why don't you try to nap?"

Callie didn't even attempt to protest. She snuggled into the sleeping bag and was fast asleep almost instantly. Jackson switched off the flashlight, and huddled in his own sleeping bag. There was no danger of him falling asleep. His thoughts would keep him wide-awake.

He'd meant every word he'd said to her. He might seem like the same person on the surface, but inside, he'd undergone a deep shift since meeting Callie.

Why, Lord? Jackson caught himself. Wow. He'd slipped into that so easily. He gave the feeling a moment to settle. *Thank You, Lord, for leading Callie to me. For putting her in my path. For using her to lead me back to You.*

As he sat there in the dark stillness, words flooded his mind, years' worth of trapped emotions, doubts, fears. They poured forth in an open, honest prayer. Tears rolled down his cheeks as he bared his soul to the One who'd made him, the One who loved him above all. By the time his thoughts and prayers began to slow, Jackson felt cleansed, as if a huge burden had lifted, and a calm descended. A new sense of purpose filled his being. And the nugget of an idea stirred in his soul.

What if he didn't have to leave Callie?

What if God had brought them together to give new direction to his life?

"Jackson, what time is it?"

Time for a change. The words filled his heart and put goose bumps on his arms. But it was not time to say anything to her yet. He had to get her out of this mess first. *Please Lord, guide me. Help me to keep Callie safe.*

Jackson glanced at his phone. "Almost ten."

Callie yawned and stretched. "I'd kill for a cup of coffee. Any idea what's up with the storm?"

Jackson dug in his duffel bag and pulled out a thermos. "Your wish is my command."

Callie's jaw dropped. "Is there anything you didn't think of?"

Yes. How hard it was going to be trapped in such tight quarters with you. "I have military and marshal training, remember? Plus I was a Boy Scout. I've learned to be prepared for anything."

"Don't care about the anything. This—" she sipped her coffee "—this is perfect." She settled back into the sleeping bag while Jackson checked the weather radar on his phone. "No one back in Texas would ever believe this if I described it."

Jackson grinned absentmindedly as he scanned the app. "Looks like the snow has stopped. Too bad I don't have an app to check the status of our pursuers. Let me poke my head out and see how it looks."

Once Jackson declared it safe to travel, Callie climbed out of the pit and into a snow globe world. She blinked at the sudden brightness. "I've never seen so much snow."

"Welcome to the Midwest in winter. It's not going to be easy walking."

"What, no snowshoes in your Mary Poppins bag?"

"I wish."

"Jackson," Callie whispered after they'd trudged along for a while. "I've been thinking. Maybe we ought to stop trying to get away and try to capture them instead."

Jackson looked at her as if she were crazy. "Do you have—"

She held up her hand to cut him off. "Hear me out. We need information. We can't just keep running forever. Apparently the DEA can't find anything, and WITSEC seems to think that just having us on the run is a solution. Maybe it's time we took action."

"Callie, my job is to protect you, not catch criminals."

She stopped and looked up at him. "Your job was to protect me so I could testify." She shrugged. "There's no longer anyone for me to testify against." She grabbed his hands and tugged on them. "Come on. Aren't you tired of being in the dark? Don't you want to know what this is all about?"

He did. But he wasn't going to risk her life to find out. "No. There are too many of them. I'm not risking your life." Especially not now.

"What do you want to do? The roads are too covered with snow to take the car, so we can't get out of here, right? But we don't know where they are, what they're doing, whether or not they stayed at the house."

"We can check that out without actually confronting them. We have to go back toward the house to get away anyway." He grinned at her. "I think you'll like our escape vehicle this time."

"Really? We have an escape vehicle? What are we using?"

"A snow boat."

Callie laughed, although her teeth were chattering in the cold. "I love how you say that as if it's the most natural thing in the world."

"It beats the choices—waiting here for them to come get us or freezing to death."

"Where are we going to get a snow boat from?"

"I've been working on one while you napped each day. Just in case we needed a way out."

"That's really cool, Jackson. Where is it?"

"That's the tricky part. It's in the barn behind the house.

We'll have to work our way back there and sneak into the barn."

They resumed the slow trudge back through the woods. "You get credit, you know," Jackson told her as they walked. "I kept thinking about how much you liked watching those ice boats. I decided to adapt it with skis."

She high-fived him.

After an hour of plodding through deep snow banks, the house came into view. Callie sighed. "It looks so warm and cozy." She shook off the longing. "So we have to find out if anyone is still here, right? Piece of cake."

Jackson laughed at her bravado. He should have known by now that she'd do whatever it took. "Or we could forget all about them and just sneak out the boat."

Callie thought about it. "I'd rather find out how many there are, take them out if we can. If I make some noise, someone will be sure to hear me and come check it out."

Jackson shook his head. "They'll probably all come out. If we're going to try to catch them at all, we need them separate." He hesitated because he didn't want to offend her. "We also need to make sure they cannot communicate with their team."

"Of course," she replied, understanding exactly what he meant. "But we don't want them to freeze to death."

Jackson eyed her with appreciation. "After all they've done to you, you can still have compassion for them?"

"I wouldn't be worth much as a person if I had no compassion for my fellow human beings, no matter how poor their choices."

"How sweet is she?"

At the sound of the new voice, Jackson swung around and found himself in the face of a shotgun muzzle. He clenched his fists and fought down his anger. They'd been so caught up in their conversation that he'd completely forgotten that the enemy might also be emerging after the storm.

"You could try showing her a little of that same compassion," Jackson suggested.

The man, dressed in a red plaid flannel shirt, gave a snort. "Not likely. Big bucks on her head."

Callie had been standing frozen in shock, but that statement released her. "Big bucks for me? Why? Why do they even care about me?"

The guy turned to answer her. "I don't know. They don't tell—"

Jackson whacked him over the back of the head with his duffel bag and down he went. "Still feeling compassionate?" he asked Callie.

"Why don't we tie him up and leave him in the snow until we lure his companion out here?"

"Should I be nervous at how much you're enjoying this? Nice work distracting him, though."

Callie laughed. "It would be if it had been intentional. But honestly, Jackson, why would anyone have money out for me? The guys I was going to testify against are dead."

"We can try to keep the other guy conscious and see what he knows."

"That's fine by me, but I don't expect he'll know any more than this fellow did. Are we going to go with my plan?"

Jackson didn't really like it, but he couldn't see any other way. "Wait until I get this one bound and gagged." He dragged the man, who was now moaning lightly. Callie took off her scarf and wrapped it around his face as a gag.

Following her example, Jackson took his own scarf and bound the man's hands behind his back to the porch railing. "We'll find a way to tie them up better once we can get in the house."

Jackson got himself hidden behind the door. Callie walked across in front of the house. She pretended to look like she was hiding, ducking between trees as she went.

The front door flew open and the other man ran out calling, "Caleb?"

Whack. Jackson took him down with the shovel he'd left by the door. They dragged him back into the house and tied him up.

While Jackson was dragging the man who was apparently named Caleb into the house, Callie grabbed supplies—helmets, goggles, sweaters, heavy gloves, anything she could find.

Jackson told her he'd call it in to the marshals and let them decide how to handle the men. "Someone from the local sheriff's office will be sent out to get them. But now, come, my lady. Your snow boat awaits."

Callie danced in delight when he opened the barn door and showed her the boat. He'd affixed ski blades to the bottom of a sailboat.

"It really is like the ice boats we saw."

"Hope it works as well. The snow up here covers the ice, so I figured skis were better than ice blades. It should work like a sailboat, but with skis."

"Very cool." Callie approved.

The snow-boat ride was fairly uneventful compared to their earlier escapes, but Callie was delighted with the way they flew across the frozen lake. This was something she wanted to try again some time.

When they reached the far shore, the roads were plowed and Jackson found someone with a car willing to drive them into town. They rented a new car and once again hit the road.

"This is starting to get old," Jackson commented as they drove.

"Not if you think about what the guy named Caleb said," Callie countered. "Neither of the two guys seemed to know why they were supposed to capture me. Jackson, did you notice they said capture—not kill? Obviously they think I know something."

"They probably think Rick either told you something or he gave you something to keep safe. Can you think of anything?"

"No. I knew nothing about this part of his life."

SEVENTEEN

"Jackson, I think I should go back to Texas." Callie paced the confines of yet another hotel suite.

"Absolutely not."

Realizing how harsh that sounded, he softened his voice. "I'm sorry. I just can't see why you would want to take that risk."

"Obviously I have something they want."

"How do you know it's in Texas?" Even as he asked, he suspected she was right.

"Since I have nothing with me from my former life— not even my poor penguin—and they're still after me, logic says there must be something back there."

Jackson bit down on his knuckle as he considered her argument. "You're presuming that the thing they want is physical, not something you know."

She shrugged. "I don't know anything that's of any use to them."

He was silent for a few minutes trying to figure out how to put this gently enough that she would take it seriously but not be scared into doing something foolish. "You have to be careful with that line of thinking, Cal. First, it's sort of a catch-22. Because you know that you know nothing, you expect they do, too. But they may think you know more than you do."

Callie nervously fingered her scarf while she considered that angle. Finally she nodded, accepting the wisdom of his thoughts.

Jackson lifted her hand and wrapped his around her fist. "You also have to consider the possibility that you do know something. When detectives, or marshals, for that matter, are putting together the pieces of a case, they always ask for every detail, no matter how small. You never know which detail, innocent on its own, will be the key to solving the mystery. You may hold a key you aren't remotely aware of."

Callie closed her eyes. "There's just no way to win this, is there?" She didn't like what he was saying. It sounded far more ominous, far more likely and far more hopeless.

"How am I supposed to figure it out, then, without telling the bad guys? How do I know what I know that matters?" She wanted to cry. "It's just giving me a headache."

Jackson wrapped his arm around her and held her tight. "That's why it's so important to tell me everything you know about the case. Even anything you may already have told Ben."

"Why. Didn't you two talk?"

"We did. But that was well over a week ago now. Besides, sometimes details get lost. Better safe—and repetitive—than sorry."

"Okay. I promise to think of anything I haven't told you. But…"

Jackson dipped his head to look at her. "But?"

"Will you be as honest with me?"

She could tell by his hesitation that he didn't want to make that promise.

"I'll agree…with a caveat. I'll be as honest as I can be, Callie. But there might be things that would jeopardize the safety of others. I can't reveal confidential information."

She didn't like it but sensed it was the best she was going to get. "If you don't think I should go home, what do you propose I do?"

"Just stay safe. Let the marshals and the DEA investigate."

That was not the answer she wanted. Callie sighed. She'd give him a day or two to see if anything changed. If not, she was going anyway.

She broke away and wandered over to the window. "Jackson, we never really talked about this. What do the officials think about Rick's involvement?"

"They think he was dealing."

He said it so matter-of-factly that Callie took a moment to process. "What?"

"I'm sorry, Callie. I know it's hard to accept."

"No, it makes sense."

"How so?"

"Because one of the things that has bothered me is that I never had any sense of him being under the influence of drugs. If we went out, he never even drank. He tended to be the sober, reliable, designated-driver sort. That makes more sense if he was dealing."

She shuddered. "It makes it a little more cold-blooded, though, doesn't it?"

Jackson waited for her to explain.

"Who was he dealing to? How much did he charge? Was I really supposed to find out about this? Or did he want me left in the dark? People who know us both wondered at what he was doing, but I didn't ask questions. That is to my eternal shame. Maybe if I had pushed, shown my displeasure…" Tears stung her eyes. "Maybe then he would be alive."

Jackson wrapped his arms fully around her and drew her into his embrace. "Callie, take it from someone who spent a decade beating himself up over not being there to change things. You couldn't have. Rick was a grown man making his own choices. Did you ever tell him that you wanted a lifestyle better than the one he could give you?"

"Of course not!" She pulled back and paced the room again. "I always told him I was happy with a simple life. I don't need things. I never wanted to accumulate possessions. All I want is the people I care about, the people who will be my family."

"And did he listen?"

She sighed heavily. "No. He was constantly planning one thing or another. He always had some new get-rich scheme. I thought I could change him. Show him a better way to live in the Lord."

She hung her head. "I knew I was failing at that, but I never imagined he'd turn to drugs—especially turning others on to them. That's a disgrace."

Jackson came and stood beside her. "I'm really sorry he wasn't smart enough to see the mistake he was making."

Callie shrugged. "The mistake was mine. Thinking he would change. Thinking he would want the same things I did."

Jackson rested his palm on her cheek. "The mistake he made was in not realizing he had the greatest blessing in you. He didn't need all those other things."

Callie didn't know how to handle such kindness so she leaned into his shoulder rather than looking up. "Thank you," she murmured against his chest.

He tipped her chin up and looked deeply into her eyes. "I wish with all my heart that we had met under other circumstances. I wouldn't have made that mistake."

Callie wanted him to kiss her. More than she wanted her next breath, more than she wanted to solve this case, she wanted him to kiss her one more time. She suspected he wanted the same thing. But she had this awful feeling that he wouldn't.

She couldn't bear the thought of never feeling his lips on hers again, so she lifted on her tiptoes and softly kissed him. Just a quick touch of her lips to his, then she drew back, whispered a thank-you and pulled away.

Jackson stood, his back rigid, as he watched her walk away and go into the other room. It was so hard to let her go, but he had no right to call her back. No right to pull her into his arms and kiss her the way he wanted to. He had to protect her, and to do that he had to put distance between them and stop wishing for what he couldn't ever have.

Or maybe he could. The idea that had been nagging at him like a woodpecker on a light pole tapped on his brain again. What if he left the Marshals? What if he went into protection with Callie and began a new life? Leaving behind all the baggage of a lost decade appealed to something deep within him. And the idea of having a future with Callie made him weak as hope fluttered through his body.

"Guide me, Lord. Show me Your way," he whispered. This praying about things was so new, it still felt shaky, and he wasn't entirely sure he was doing it right. But a sense of peace had invaded his being lately, even in the midst of all this chaos. That had to mean something.

He couldn't say anything to her yet. Wouldn't make promises he might not be able to keep. First priority still was keeping her safe and alive. His boss had decided to keep her in WITSEC for the time being at least. The defendants might be dead, but someone was clearly still after her. They might need her, so she had to be kept safe.

He glanced at his phone, debating calling in for a report. The date jumped out at him. December 31. New Year's Eve.

Perfect. A shiver of expectation ran down his arms.

He might not be able to say anything, but they could end the year in style and begin the new one as he hoped to go on—together.

"Callie." He raised a hand to knock on her door, but the sound of muffled sobs stilled it midair. He rested his head against the door, pleading silently. *Don't cry, sweetheart. It will all work out.* He clenched his fist, resisting the urge to go in and hold her. "Cal, I'm going out to pick up dinner. Anything special you want?"

He heard her sniffle and attempt to clear her throat. "No, thanks. I'm not very hungry."

Callie heard the suite door close behind him and sat up. Forget waiting two days. He wasn't going to change his mind. She needed to leave now, while he was gone.

She quickly added a few pieces of clothing to her go bag and headed for the door. No. She couldn't go without leaving him a note. He'd been too good to her and she knew he'd blame himself.

There was no doubt he'd also come after her the minute he noticed her gone, so she resorted to the oldest trick in the book. She plumped up pillows and drew the comforter over them. For a final touch, she arranged the edge of one of her sweaters so it was hanging out the side. She tucked her note to him on the pillow under the blanket and stuck a second note to the bedroom door. *I need some time alone. Please don't disturb.*

Hopefully this would work long enough so she had time to get away. He'd immediately know where she was going, so her only hope was in buying time and taking an unusual route.

Callie took one last look around the room before closing the door behind her. She had to fight back tears at the thought of never seeing Jackson again. Leaving him was hard. Knowing he'd feel betrayed was even worse. Her eyes stung as she ran down the back stairs and ducked out the service entrance. His words echoed in her mind. He'd made it clear there was no future for them, no way to be together. She had to do this.

She hated to admit even to herself, but she might have given up on her quest for justice if he'd given her even a hint that they could be a couple, that they could build a family together. This bitter leaving was payback for her character weakness. As she'd written in her note, justice was all that mattered now.

She couldn't leave Jackson without a car, so Callie called a taxi to take her to the bus station. She had to stop for a minute and think where they were. After leaving Vermont, they'd driven south and west and had ended up in western Pennsylvania. But then they'd headed into central Pennsylvania to the safe house. She had two options: west to Pittsburgh or southeast to Philadelphia. Jackson would assume she was heading south, so she bought a ticket west. If she could get to Pittsburgh, she could catch a flight to Texas.

EIGHTEEN

Crowds were gathering, everyone dressed in their finest party clothes, as Jackson made his way through the hotel lobby. Dare they come down and join the celebration? No. He wouldn't risk it. He really didn't want to anyway. The thought of ringing in the New Year with just Callie made his heart sing with joy.

If only he could tell her his plans, ask what she thought. Make sure she felt the same. But he vowed to say nothing until the case was done. They couldn't risk the distraction.

Jackson used the key card to open the door. He made sure it shut tightly behind him. As excited as a boy on Christmas morning, he set out the groceries and party foods he'd bought and called out for Callie. When there was no response, he walked over to her door.

And came up against a sign asking that he leave her alone.

The sign was like a bucket of ice water, dousing his hopes and plans for a fun evening. Dejected, he returned to the kitchenette and stored the food in the tiny refrigerator. Midnight was still several hours off. Maybe he'd follow her lead and take a nap so he was fresh for the celebration.

Noise from the revelry downstairs jolted him awake hours later as the crowd counted down. "Ten, nine…"

Jackson jumped up and dashed to Callie's door. He knocked, and when there was no response, he cracked the door and peered in. Disappointment swamped him as he noted she was still sleeping soundly. He closed the door and went back into the living room.

New Year's Eve was a lonely time when you were all by yourself. He knew that from too many years of experience. He'd thought, hoped, that this year would be different. Spending New Year's with the one he loved. Yes, he loved Callie. He knew that now. He'd hoped tonight would be the first of many New Year's Eves they'd spend together.

Jackson flipped on the television and vicariously enjoyed the celebration. He dozed fitfully, and when he woke at three, he decided to check on Callie again.

He cracked the door. She hadn't moved.

Had not moved. No one slept like that. Suspicions gnawed at his gut. Had he really been that stupid?

No, he'd trusted her. *I don't lie*, she'd said. He looked at the sign on the door. Technically not a lie, but that didn't really matter to him as he crossed the floor and pulled the blanket back.

Pillows tumbled to the floor and Jackson sank down on the bed with a groan. He buried his face in his hands. "Oh, Callie. What did you do?"

When he opened his eyes, he saw her note sitting on the pillow. Bracing himself for what it would say, he lifted the paper and carried it into the other room where he could see.

Dear Jackson,
Please don't follow me.

Thank you for everything you have done. I know you'll say it's just your job, but the caring and attention you gave me went far above and beyond just a job and I will always be grateful to God for putting you in my life at the time I needed you most. You've built my courage, showed me how to protect myself and reinforced my belief that justice must prevail.

Justice is more important than my life right now. Not for revenge, not for my sake, but so these men are stopped before any more naive children are introduced to drugs, before any more innocent lives are lost. If I can stop them, then even if my life is lost in the process, I will have accomplished something worthy. Please don't follow me. I don't want you to try to stop me and I don't want the burden of endangering your life.

Thank you for reminding me that there are honorable men in this world, men who are truly worthy of love.

Yours, Callie

PS—I apologize for any professional embarrassment I've caused you. I have to do what I know is right.

Jackson slammed his fist on the bed. Regret ripped through him. She didn't have a clue what she was walking into.

And whose fault was that?

He grabbed his phone and tried calling her, but it went straight to voice mail. He dialed his boss next and paced the room while he listened to Logan's phone ring.

"Walker, it's three a.m. This had better be good."

"It's actually pretty bad, sir." Jackson swallowed his pride. "My witness ran away." He held the phone away from his ear to save his hearing. When Logan had calmed enough, he explained the situation.

It was little comfort to hear his boss tell him he'd done nothing wrong. He had. He'd done the one thing that was unacceptable in WITSEC. He'd lost his witness.

"I'm sure she's heading for Austin, so I'll be on the

next flight out." He had no intention of trying to track her. His only chance at stopping her was to get there faster. "If you can get some marshals at the airports or train stations, maybe we can get her before she goes to her house."

Callie knew Jackson would probably have people waiting at the airports in Austin, so she'd bought a ticket to San Antonio instead. Once she landed there, she rented a car and began the drive.

She had to push Jackson from her thoughts and concentrate on why she had come home, but that was easier said than done. Somewhere along Route 35, north of San Marcos but still south of Austin, Callie fell apart. Being back in Texas brought reminders of her previous life, of all she had lost.

She tried hard not to think of Jackson because it hurt too much. How was it possible to care so much for someone you'd known for such a short period of time? Better that she think about the case and why someone would be after her. What did Rick have or know? She tried to recall everything she'd told Jackson about Rick, hoping something would click, but that only made her wallow in self-pity thinking about the differences between the men.

It was so easy now for her to see that she'd never really loved Rick. Loving Jackson taught her the difference between affection, and a deep and abiding love.

There, she'd let herself acknowledge it. Against all wisdom, she'd gone and fallen in love with her marshal. Jackson had become a part of her forever. Wherever she went in her life, a little piece of her heart would always be left behind with him. It just about killed her to think that she wouldn't ever know what happened in his life.

Tears started flowing again as she considered the injustice of it and all they had lost.

It had been different with Rick. She saw that now. He hadn't really wanted her. He'd wanted the image of them he'd created—the wealthy, young, hip, new-generation Texan. Lots of land, lots of money, all the best of everything. She thought of the model house he had given her in her classroom one day, promising that someday it would be theirs. She'd thought it was ugly. She wanted something small with a white picket fence and a garden.

He'd responded that the house was her security. "You remember that, Callie darlin'," he'd said. "If anything should ever happen to me, that house is your security."

Goose bumps rose along her arms and nerves shivered down her spine. Was that it? Was that where he'd hidden whatever it was the men wanted?

Thankfully the road was fairly empty because her thoughts were consumed with this new idea. She was pretty sure now. The timing had been right. The more she thought on it, the more certain she was. She wanted so badly to call Jackson and tell him. But what if she was wrong? What if there was nothing there? Worse still, what if he tried to stop her from checking?

Callie drove around the block twice to make sure no one was following her. She'd driven by earlier, but the school had been crowded with families here for Football Fiesta.

She was sad to have missed that. The New Year's Day tradition of celebrating the high school's football team was always a highlight of the school year, a chance for the whole community to have one more football celebration before hanging up the helmets and cleats until next season.

The fiesta was over now. Only scattered streamers and balloons remained. The parking lot was empty, so she parked her rental car in a shopping center down the street so as not to draw attention. She strolled casually along the sidewalk until she got to the school. She stayed in the shadows and approached her classroom to look in the window. It was too dark to see in, but that didn't keep emotion from overcoming her.

She sank down on the grass, leaning against the brick wall, and buried her face in her hands. But she pulled herself together quickly; she didn't have time to think about this now, time to grieve for all she'd lost. She had to get inside the school.

She tried the front door, but it was locked. She'd been afraid of that. Too bad she didn't have keys anymore.

Waiting until the next day was not an option, not with Jackson likely on her heels and who knew who else chasing her. Callie glanced nervously over her shoulder. Whoever they were, they seemed to have an uncanny ability to discover her location even without the tracker. She'd felt safer when Jackson was with her.

The urge to call him, to hear his voice, swamped Callie. Maybe he could help her get into the school. Surely he'd forgive her...

Maybe not. Knowing he would more likely try to talk her out of her plan stifled the inclination. She could try Ben instead. She remembered Ben putting his number on her speed dial back in New York before all of this began. Jackson had said something about him being back in Texas. Maybe he could help.

She ducked behind the garden wall to place the call, but Ben didn't answer. She left a voice message, telling him she was headed to the school and to call right away if he got the message.

Now what to do? Panic threatened. Why hadn't she even thought about the school being locked? She'd been so intent on getting here that she hadn't even considered the most important thing.

Surely she hadn't gotten this far to fail now. *I am the Lord, your God, who takes hold of your right hand and says to you, Do not fear; I will help you.*

Callie breathed softly, allowing God's love to flow over her. She wasn't sure if the verse from Isaiah applied to when you were intentionally doing something risky, but she chose to believe it did. She focused on breathing and thinking calmly. There must be a way in; she just had to think about it. All those nights she'd been here late…

Yes! The cleaning crew was notorious for leaving a back door ajar so they could go out for smoke breaks.

Callie checked again to make sure she was alone. Then she sneaked through the garden and around the back. Sure enough, there was the door with just the smallest piece of cardboard stuck in to keep it from locking. She silently rejoiced at the payoff for all those nights and sank to her knees in thanks.

Because she was on her knees already, she took a moment to pray. *Dear Lord, help me to find what I need. Help me to be able to locate the evidence to stop these people from hurting anyone else.*

Callie didn't want anyone who was cleaning to notice her movement, so she crawled along the wall toward the door. Once there, she eased it open and peered down the hall. Loud music was playing in the gym at the far end. The maintenance cart with its mops and brooms and cleaning supplies was parked outside the door. Good. They'd be there awhile cleaning all the debris. If she was quick, she should be able to make it as far as the cross hall before anyone came out.

She didn't think the janitors would say anything, but doubts plagued her. Could they have been involved, too? Could they have had anything to do with her classroom being trashed?

No. She had to stop doing this. She couldn't see everyone as a suspect. How could she even live like that? That's what Jackson's life was like. A wave of remorse washed over her. She wished she could have given him a respite from that, been a haven so he had someone in his life to love and trust.

Wiping her eyes, she concentrated on making her way to her classroom. When she opened the door and slipped inside unnoticed, another wave of homesickness engulfed her, a longing for her old life in this room. She had built a community here, created a safe haven for her children from all the troubles of their young lives.

She allowed herself a few minutes to wander the room, trailing a hand over a desk, stroking a favorite book. The new teacher had made some changes, and that hurt because it emphasized the permanence of her being gone.

Tears clogged her throat when she spied the life-sized penguin perched in the rocking chair, but it also prompted her to get a move on. There would be time later for sentimental memories. She was here to do a job.

A quick scan of the room told her the new teacher—or some official—had removed her belongings. Where could they have put them? She checked the closet, hoping to find at least some of her things, but nothing of hers was there. Her stomach cramped as she realized that of course they would have removed her stuff. They'd probably done that when the room was trashed, if not before.

Or had the bad guys found the model house?

With a sinking feeling, she had to acknowledge that possibility.

Except none of her personal things were here. So hopefully the janitors had just moved everything. Did she dare ask them? She heaved a sigh. Maybe Jackson had been right about not doing this on her own. She was in so far over her head. But that made it sink-or-swim time. She'd have to take her chances with the men she knew.

Callie ran down the hall to where she had seen them and knocked on the door. The smiles that beamed from all three faces reassured her they were happy to see her. There wasn't even the glimmer of anything but joy, so she spent a few precious minutes speaking with them. It was a balm to her soul to hear them say how sorry they were for her troubles. Their gentle kindness was reassuring. This was her world, the world she had built of warm, loving people who looked out for each other. How had it all gone so wrong?

She explained to them that she was in a hurry because it probably wasn't safe for her to be here. When she asked about her belongings, they assured her everything was safe in boxes in the basement.

Manny, the custodian she had known the longest, insisted on helping her. Callie was scared, but she reassured herself. She'd never been afraid of him before. How many nights had she worked late while these men cleaned? They would always stop by and chat with her as they swept her classroom and the hallway. They were a part of the school family. How sad was it that Rick had made her lose trust in everyone?

She allowed Manny to help her find the boxes and promised to tell him if she needed any help, but she was relieved when he left her alone in the basement. Truth be told, once she'd set aside her fears, she'd been glad to have him help her find her way. The basement was a maze of rooms ranging from storage space to the boiler room, assorted workshops to vast empty spaces that were meant to be used as a shelter in an emergency. It was confusing under the best of circumstances. No wonder it was off-limits during the school day.

Half an hour slid by as she dug through boxes of her life. Memories assaulted her of happier times spent with her children. Each piece of her life that she removed from a box held a story. How many of them held clues?

She was dusty, tired and thirsty. And she wanted Jackson.

Deciding to give in to temptation, she took out her phone, only to realize there was no signal this far back in the basement. She wandered the room, holding her phone up, and when it finally showed bars, she called. Tears of frustration welled when he didn't answer. She left a message telling him she was down in the elementary school basement, had called Ben once and was going to call him again.

She dialed Ben's number and waited until she heard it begin to ring. The ringing echoed throughout the basement. Callie held the phone out from her ear and listened, then snapped it shut.

Ben's phone was ringing in the basement. He was down here with her.

NINETEEN

Callie's nerves pricked. Why was Ben down here? Why had he shown up without calling to say he was coming? Something felt off. When she'd left the message, she hadn't even known she'd be coming to the basement. How had he known she was here?

Maybe the custodial staff had alerted him. But wouldn't they have escorted him as they'd done with her?

Instinct prompted her to hide until she could figure this out. She set her phone on vibrate and edged toward the back stairs. She might just be jittery because of everything that was going on. Though she tried to write it off as that, her gut said this was different.

Her phone vibrated. *Please let it be Jackson.* It was Ben. She answered cautiously. "Hello?"

"Hey, Callie. Where are you? I got your message so I figured I'd come help."

Callie tried to feel reassured by that. He was the marshal who'd been in charge of protecting her originally. She really shouldn't have any reason not to trust him.

"I'm down in the cellar."

"Hang tight. I'll be right down."

Callie crouched behind some boxes. Was it possible she'd heard his phone from outside? She took some slow breaths, tried to calm down while she waited for him.

Her phone began to vibrate again. Jackson. Relief washed over her.

"Man, am I glad you—"

He cut her off. "Callie, listen carefully, did you call Ben?"

"Yes, he's here now."

Jackson's intake of breath came through the phone. That wasn't encouraging.

"There? Can he hear me?"

"No," she whispered.

"Don't trust him. Try to get away from him." She could envision him clenching his phone, biting back his temper. "It's important, Callie."

"But, Jackson, I've almost got the evidence. I know where it is."

"Wait for me to get there."

"Ben's coming. He said he'd help."

She heard a rush of indrawn breath. "Callie, I think Ben is a mole. I think he's the reason we were being followed all the time."

Callie was frantic. "What should I do?" she whispered into the phone. "I can hear him coming."

"Is there anywhere to hide?"

"I'm in the basement of the school. I've never been down here before. I don't know. It looks like a lot of empty rooms."

"Callie?"

"He's here," she whispered into the phone.

"I know. I heard him. Okay, he doesn't know that you suspect anything, so maybe you're better off just playing along. Whatever you do, don't let him find the real evidence."

Or he'll have no reason to keep you alive. Those were

the unspoken words Callie heard. She knew they were what Jackson was thinking.

"Where are you? I don't know how long I can put him off."

"I just landed at the airport. I'll have security send backup. Hopefully they'll get there before I do."

"Callie?" Ben's voice was starting to sound impatient.

She held the phone away and called out. "I'm back here, Ben. I'll be right out. I was just looking for something."

"Okay."

"Jackson? I've got to go. He's getting suspicious."

"Callie, wait, love. Don't hang up. Keep the phone on in your pocket or something. I'll be able to hear what's going on and relay it to the police."

She sighed deeply, feeling immensely comforted to know he would be close in some way. "Okay."

"I'm praying for you, my brave lady."

That warmed her heart even more.

Callie grabbed some old drawings she'd had in her hand when she'd come looking for a phone signal and made her way out to the main room. "Hey, Ben. I'm so glad you got my message. I tried reaching Jackson, but he didn't answer his phone either."

"Callie. You're looking good, sweetie."

"You're the one who's looking good." It wasn't hard to feign concern. She had been worried about him for a long time. "Are you okay? I feel so awful that you took a hit meant for me."

He gave her a quick hug and she tried not to cringe. "That's my job, dear. Did you leave Jackson a message?"

She made a face but didn't directly answer. "Jackson and I didn't part on exactly the best of terms."

That was enough to distract him from the fact that she hadn't answered his question. Knowing that Jackson was listening, she said, "He said it was too dangerous for me to come back here, but I thought I knew better. I wanted to find the evidence we need."

"Why did he think it was dangerous?" Knowing Jackson's suspicions, Callie recognized the tension in Ben's voice.

"He figured the men who were after me would have a better chance of finding me if I came back to Texas. He wanted me to leave it to your office to figure things out."

"But you're here."

She grimaced. "Like I said, I had a different idea. I figured if I came here and could look through my stuff, it might spark some idea of what Rick was hiding."

"Did it?"

Callie shrugged. She didn't want to lie, but she was not going to aid a criminal. "It never occurred to me that my stuff would be boxed away. I had to ask the custodians to find the boxes for me. Manny brought me down and dug things out."

"Is he still down here?"

His questions added to Callie's nerves. Was she hearing things in his voice because she was nervous, or was he really a threat? She had to fight the tremble in her own voice as she replied.

"I told them to let me look on my own first. It's going to be sort of emotional, you know." She forced some tears, which wasn't all that hard. "I mean this is the first time I've seen any of this stuff since before Rick was killed. I'm still having such a hard time dealing with it all and trying to understand him and why he got involved in this."

Ben wandered around the room, as if looking for something himself. "What did Jackson tell you?"

"Not much. He really didn't seem to know any more

about it than I do. What makes a man go bad, Ben? Why did Rick turn from the man I knew?"

Did Ben flinch at her question? She could only imagine how Jackson had reacted to it if he was still on the phone, but she needed some sense of where she stood with Ben.

"I don't know, Callie. I guess it depends on the man. Some have a bad streak that's hidden. Others, well, maybe they just don't care about anyone but themselves."

Those were definitely odd comments. "I don't really think either of those fit Rick, but I guess I'll never know now."

"Where are your boxes? I'll help you look."

Putting on her best pouty face, Callie said, "I was just about to go look for some water. Couldn't it wait until I get back?"

"No. Let's do it now."

Callie cringed at his sharp tone as much as his words. "Ben, I really don't feel well. It's stuffy down here. I need to get some air and water."

Ben's gaze shifted around the room. His hand stayed firmly in his back pocket. "You'll be fine as soon as we find the evidence. We don't have time to waste. You don't know how soon they'll catch up to us."

Panic swirled in her belly, and she thought she might save herself for real by getting sick on Ben's feet. Stall. Jackson had told her to stall.

"Okay, but if I pass out, it's your fault."

The glare that comment caused in no way resembled the face of the caring man she'd spent weeks working with last fall. She wanted to ask what had happened. Survival instincts kept her mute.

"The boxes are in here, the far room away from the furnace." She added the last for Jackson's benefit.

Ben forced her to go ahead of him. Still the hand didn't

leave his pocket. She was beginning to worry about what was in there. *Silly.* She wanted to smack herself. *He's a federal marshal. Of course he has a gun.* That wasn't very reassuring.

"So what are we looking for?" he asked as she settled down beside a box.

Callie shrugged. "Beats me. Jackson thought there might be something here to identify the thugs who killed Rick. Or at least the ones coming after me since the first ones are already dead."

"You look, and I'll stand guard. Hurry."

Callie sorted through the pile of papers in the box closest to the door. She already knew there was nothing in there but old writing samples. What she was looking for was a model house. It wouldn't be with papers. It was far more likely to be on a shelf somewhere. She scanned the room and her gaze lit on a turret sticking out from behind the steam pipe. Shifting a little, she could see the rest of the model house, the one that looked more like a museum piece than a potential home.

"Ben, I'm about to give up. Maybe there was nothing. Maybe they're wrong, and Rick didn't know anything."

"They're not wrong."

Callie flinched. That was not Ben's voice. Who else was down here?

Jackson's hands froze on the steering wheel. He strained to hear what was going on, but the sounds were muffled. Once Ben had insisted Callie walk into the other room to search, the signal had weakened. He'd heard the new voice, though. Who was there besides Ben?

Traffic was moving at a snail's pace, and Jackson pounded on the wheel. Not that it did any good, but it was an outlet for frustration and the fear he wouldn't admit to.

He muted his phone, rested it on the seat beside him and grabbed for the burner phone he was using to communicate with his office so he didn't lose Callie.

"Walker here. There's a problem. Someone else just showed up in the school basement."

Jackson listened carefully and chills started at the base of his spine. "Are you sure alerting DEA was a good idea? You might want to ask for more backup. I just heard someone else arrive, and he didn't sound like he was on our side."

Jackson clicked off the phone and focused back on Callie. Being able to hear her voice calmed him a bit, but it also triggered questions. Why had she gone off without him? She knew the danger. Why hadn't she waited?

The answer to his questions smacked him across the side of the head with the force of an oak tree. He'd told Callie he would have the sense not to make the same mistake as Rick, but he had. He'd let her get away. He thought back to all the signs she'd given him, how she'd asked him to help her. But he'd been so frozen with fear of losing her that he'd pushed her away. And because of that, because of him, she was in mortal danger.

"Lord, help me to get to her. You know what's happening. I don't have a good feeling about it. Please help me, Lord. Help me get to her in time."

Fear such as he'd never known pressed on Jackson. He couldn't lose her, not now. Not when he was ready to take the chance and commit fully to a life with her.

Traffic eased. Jackson hit the gas and sped down the darkened streets. His GPS was talking to him, telling him what turns to make. He was surprised she didn't tell him to slow down because she could barely keep up. "Make a left, make a right. Recalculating."

There, up ahead, he could see the school. Lights flooded

the parking lot. Jackson pulled the car to a stop and jumped out, flashing his badge at anyone who tried to stop him.

He reached the barricade in minutes. "Who's in charge here?"

The local officer stepped forward, and Jackson introduced himself. "What's the status?"

"Nothing's wrong here. We're sending cars home. The custodian said a former teacher wanted to check her files. The US marshal and the DEA agent from her case went in to help her. Not sure why we were called in."

"Has anyone spoken with her?" Jackson asked.

"Negative. The lead officer spoke with the DEA agent upon arrival."

No. This was all wrong. Callie wouldn't—

A scream rent the air.

"Where did that come from?" the officer asked.

"My phone." Jackson's body went rigid as he brought his emotions under control. "That was the teacher. I'm going in. I need backup. I have good reason to believe that at least one of those federal agents has turned and is a threat to the teacher."

The officer paled. "Done." He signaled to several officers clustered by the cars. "Go with him. Do what he tells you."

Jackson didn't like going in with only a few unknown officers, but he didn't have time to wait for backup that might not be coming. He quickly filled the cops in on what he needed from them, explaining that Callie needed to be protected at all costs. They donned bulletproof vests and headed toward the school building.

Jackson wished he dared talk to Callie. He wanted to reassure her he was coming in, but the danger of someone else overhearing was too great.

When they reached the school and crouched beside the

wall, he asked the officers, "Do any of you know the layout of this school?"

One of the younger men spoke out. "I attended elementary school here. Can't say I've ever been in the basement, but I know the upper floor rooms."

Jackson scanned the throng of people that had gathered in the darkness. "Wait here a minute," he told the officers. "I'm going to see what the head custodian can tell me." He crossed over to where the custodians were standing and hurriedly exchanged words.

Once he had the layout embedded in his brain, he felt a bit better. He gathered his team in a huddle and drew a rough floor plan in the gravel. "Callie's last identifiable location was the back room far from the furnace. I think that's this one. Good news is there's an outside staircase that leads into it."

He studied the crude map for a few minutes. "I think we need to split up. Half of us can go down the back stairwell, and another five can go through the building. Don't do anything unless you hear from me." A thought crossed his mind.

"Do any of you have trouble with the idea of shooting at a dirty cop if it becomes necessary?"

Jackson took a crucial moment to stare into the eyes of each man as he answered. He needed to know they were all on the same side. "Okay, then."

"One more scream like that, and they'll find your bones when they tear this place down."

Callie shrugged. She'd only screamed so that Jackson could hear there was trouble. "I know you, don't I? You came to see me with Ben in New York. To ask me questions about Rick. You glared at me because I didn't know anything."

He nodded, and Callie realized he had no intention of letting her leave here alive, scream or no scream. He was the DEA agent who had rescued the assistant US attorney. Had stopped the kidnapping.

Of course. Because the kidnappers didn't know the change of plans, but he did, so he'd stopped them from taking the wrong person. And now he had the right person. Terror coursed through Callie, turning her insides to jelly. She leaned back against the pile of boxes and prayed.

She was trying not to be afraid. *Please, Lord. Help me know what to do. Help me make the most of this.*

The pile of boxes shifted under her. An idea began to take shape. She'd distract them and get the answers she wanted at the same time.

She looked him straight in the eye. Yup, same bright blue eyes she remembered. "What did you want me to say that day in New York?"

"The same thing I want from you now. Where did that stupid boyfriend of yours hide the papers?"

"What papers?"

"Don't play dumb with me." He was losing patience, and for a moment Callie was afraid he would strike her.

Ben spoke up, his tone calm compared to his colleague's. "Callie, Rick stole papers from some important people. Do you know about them?"

Finally. "So that's what this has been about? All this tracking and attempting to get to me?"

Ben nodded. "He made some people really angry."

She smirked. "I guess so, given all the trouble you've gone to. Hate to burst your bubble, but I don't know a thing about any papers. If you haven't figured it out by now, I was apparently the last person Rick would have confided in." That realization didn't sting as much as it should have.

She had Jackson to thank for that. He'd shown her how a real man, an everyday hero, behaved.

The DEA agent clearly didn't like her answer. Ben put a restraining hand on his arm, but he quickly shook it off and headed toward her. "Even if he didn't tell you, he must have left the papers with you. We've searched everywhere else."

Anger filled Callie. "You! You're the one who trashed my classroom." She didn't care that he'd done it to her home, as well. The idea of this man touching the things her precious children used each day set her pulse pounding. She glared at him as she clenched and unclenched her fists to keep from clawing at him. The only thing that kept her rooted to the spot was knowing she would need this pile of boxes to help her escape.

"Maybe if you tell me what is in the papers, rather than threaten me, I could think of someplace he might have hidden them."

"Do you think I'm an idiot?" the agent asked.

Callie shrugged. "You tell me." She was deliberately provoking him and it worked. He charged.

At the very last minute, she stepped to the side and gave the teetering pile of boxes a shove. They toppled over onto him, knocking him back.

Callie didn't wait to see what would happen. She took off, rushing past a stunned Ben and heading into the maze of basement rooms.

A shot sounded behind her and a bullet slammed into the concrete wall by her head. She quickly ducked into another room and searched for someplace to hide.

The room was empty, but it led into another beyond it. She'd become so disoriented, she wasn't sure if she was running deeper into the school or heading toward the exterior. Footsteps behind her warned there was no choice but to keep moving. She dashed across the room and into the vast open space of the shelter room.

Not a good choice.

Jackson froze when he heard the shot. *Please, Lord. Protect my Callie.* He held up a hand to stop the men behind him. Half of them he directed to round the perimeter of the school and go down the stairs by the boiler room. The sound of the shot was from deeper inside, so she apparently had moved. He was taking the rest of the men and heading in through the building.

Once inside, they proceeded quickly from classroom to classroom, scanning each to make sure no one was hidden inside. Jackson kicked confetti as he walked, and he was reminded of Callie describing the parties with her students. Sadness swamped him, but he shoved it away. No time for emotion now.

Another shot. It felt like it had come from directly beneath his feet. According to the head custodian, the entry to the basement should be up ahead on the right. Jackson opened the door and gestured for the men to wait before following. He edged his way down the stairs, step by step, taking care to make no noise and listening for any clue of Callie's whereabouts.

"Thought you'd get away, did you?"

Jackson halted. That sounded like the man whose voice he'd heard over the phone.

"It was worth a try."

Jackson thought his knees might buckle at the sound of Callie's voice, and he realized just how deeply he'd feared he'd never hear her again. Energy surged though him and he crept closer. She was so near now.

The sight that greeted him at the bottom of the stairs

made his heart skip a beat. Callie stood against the far wall. A man with huge federal letters emblazoned on his back stood facing her, his gun leveled at her head.

Her eyes widened as she saw Jackson step into the room. He placed a finger over his mouth to warn her to silence, but it was too late. The agent picked up on her reaction and swirled around to point his gun at Jackson. He fired off a shot, but the distance was too great and it hit the concrete to the right of Jackson's head. He dodged the spray of concrete and rolled behind one of the supporting columns. He leveled his own weapon, but there was no straight shot that didn't include the possibility of hitting Callie.

The agent moved swiftly and grabbed Callie from behind. He wrapped his arms around her and held the gun to her head. "Drop your weapon."

Jackson could barely hear him over the sound of blood rushing in his head. He hadn't come this far to lose her now. *Dear Lord, if ever You have an ear for a sinner, hear me now. I don't deserve Your help, but Callie does. I know I shouldn't be bargaining, but please, please help her.*

Another shot rang out, and Jackson froze.

One long terrible moment passed before the agent crumpled to the ground. Callie broke from his grasp and ran for Jackson. He jumped up and pulled her behind the column. He wanted nothing more than to wrap her in his arms forever, but because he had no idea where the shot had come from, he was taking no chances.

He scanned the room, but there was no one in sight. Had one of the other officers come to his rescue?

Shielding Callie with his body, he hurried to the stairs.

"No need to run, Jackson."

For the second time that evening, Jackson went still

as a statue. He turned, taking care to keep Callie behind him. Ben stood hunched over, gasping for breath, blood streaming from a cut on his head.

"What happened to you?" Jackson asked.

Ben ignored the question as he leaned over the agent to check for a pulse, then tossed his own weapon aside. "I'm still on your side. You have nothing to fear from me."

Callie slumped against his back. Jackson's body wanted to do the same, but too many days of suspicion made him unable to surrender trust so easily. He kept his gun trained on his mentor. "Talk, Ben."

"Can you call EMS first? He shot at me when I tried to stop him. I think I need…" He slumped to the ground.

"Was there anyone else down here?" Jackson whispered to Callie.

"No."

"Okay." He shouted up the stairs to the police officers to stay at attention but call for medical help. "You wait here," he told Callie. "I'm going to check on Ben."

"Not on your life."

He rolled his eyes. That was Callie. Even in danger, she would argue with him.

He wanted to believe that Ben was a good marshal. He wanted faith in his mentor restored, but Jackson was taking no chances with Callie's life. "Stay back until I'm sure he's not up to something."

Noise at the top of the stairs alerted him to the arrival of medical help, who must have been just outside in the parking lot. Calling to them to wait, he walked over to his friend, looked him straight in the eye and patted him down for other weapons. The resigned sadness in Ben's eyes told him he understood. He grabbed for Jackson's arm and whispered, "Sorry…I can explain."

Jackson stared at him, his tension easing as he saw past

today to the man he had known for so many years. "It can wait." He squeezed Ben's hand and called out to EMS that they could come down now.

Callie came up beside Jackson and slipped her hand into his as she bent to kiss Ben's cheek. "You saved my life. Thank you."

Jackson squeezed her hand, then let go and wrapped his arm tightly around her. His voice was hoarse as he echoed her words.

They stepped back to let EMS get to work. Jackson kept his arm wrapped tightly around Callie. He didn't know what to say so he just held her and offered prayers of thanks. *Dear Lord, from the bottom of my heart, I thank You. I don't know what the future brings, but thank You for today and for saving Callie.*

"Come on," he told her. "Let's go."

"No. Wait."

Jackson stopped and took a deep breath. Would this woman ever stop arguing?

"I need to show you something." She took his hand and led him deeper into the basement. All around them, police officers hustled, securing the site, but she walked on.

She led him into a room that looked like a tornado had ripped through. Boxes were flung every which way. She stepped through the mess and reached to pull a model house from behind a pole.

She walked back to him, holding it up triumphantly. "This may be what they wanted."

"A toy house?"

Callie laughed and the sound was such sweet balm to his soul. "Apparently Rick hid something in here." A frown furrowed her brow as she peered in the windows. "At least I think he did."

"Let's take it upstairs and examine it where there's some light."

"Wait, Jackson. What's this?

Callie had been examining the front door and found a board loose. She pried it up and pulled out a key wrapped in a piece of paper. She unfurled the paper to see a bunch of coffee stains and a series of numbers. "Great," she muttered. "Another puzzle."

"No, that's good. It's a locker number and combination. We just have to figure out where it is."

"Wouldn't they have checked everywhere he would have been likely to have something?"

"Yup, that's why we have to think."

Callie sighed. "I could really use a cup of coff—" Goose bumps rose on her arms and shivers ran in circles up her legs. "Jackson, that's it. Let me see the paper."

"What?"

"There's a place downtown that Rick and I used to meet for coffee all the time. Right next door is one of those mailbox places where you can rent a box or a storage locker. This napkin, half the logo is missing, but it's from that coffee shop. Rick must have rented a locker there."

Jackson tipped her chin up so he could stare once more into her beautiful eyes. "See, you did know the answer all along."

Before she could respond, he leaned in and kissed her.

Callie paced the marshals' office. Where was Jackson? Surely he'd come to say goodbye. He wouldn't just abandon her without even wishing her well, would he?

Honestly, she didn't know. He'd acted so strangely in the past few days since they'd found the locker and discovered a treasure trove of money, recordings and papers Rick had collected. It was enough to put that gang away for a lifetime.

Callie tried to be satisfied with the knowledge that she'd achieved her goal. Justice had been meted out. The bad guys were locked up, at least this set of them. There would always be more criminals for people like Jackson to deal with, more witnesses to protect, but at least she could enter her new life knowing she'd found justice for Rick.

Another consolation was understanding Ben's role. The DEA agent, Quint, had blackmailed Ben when he discovered some problems the marshal was having with his son. Ben had asked for Jackson to replace him guarding Callie as a way of buying time to keep her safe. Jackson hadn't been happy to have been kept in the dark on that, but he'd get over it.

"Callie, it's time to go." The new marshal was holding out an envelope. "Jackson asked me give you this. He said you'd understand when you read it."

Callie wasn't sure she would be able to read through the tears filling her eyes, but she opened the envelope and pulled out the single card.

"For I know the plans I have for you," says the Lord. "They are plans for good and not for evil, to give you a future and a hope."
Never lose hope, Callie. I love you.
Jackson

He wasn't coming. She understood that. The quote from Jeremiah touched her heart, but she couldn't focus past the fact that Jackson wasn't coming to see her off. She touched a finger to her lips, remembering that last kiss. Apparently that had been goodbye. She swallowed hard. It wasn't like she wasn't used to things ending badly.

"Tell him goodbye for me when you see him."

* * *

Jackson stood at the window watching her go. He'd known he couldn't talk to her without giving away his plan. If he were going to join her in witness protection, he would have to wrap up everything in his old life. That would take time. He couldn't risk her arguing and trying to stay with him.

He watched her step into the car and blew her a kiss. 'Soon, Cal," he whispered through the glass. "If everything goes according to plan. God be with you."

TWENTY

"Thank you, Lord, for this glorious spring day."

Callie walked out onto her porch and breathed deeply of the cool Kentucky air. The view was breathtaking, endless acres of bluegrass swaying in the morning breeze. All that was missing was the horses. Maybe someday.

And Jackson.

Tears welled in her eyes, but she swiped them away. All these months later and thoughts of him still made emotion swell in her heart. Would she ever learn to be truly happy here?

She could be—so very happy—if only Jackson were with her.

He'd made this happen for her; she knew it. But what did it mean without him?

She tried to push away the thoughts of him, focusing instead on all she had to be grateful for. She was alive. She had her dream home, if not the family to go with it. In time she would figure out a way to make something of her life.

At least she prayed she would. When things were really bad, she prayed through song. At least out here, away from everything, she could once more sing to her heart's content.

She stepped off the porch and wandered across the back lawn. Early-morning sunlight streamed through the trees and shone down on her. She started singing—softly at first—the song that always filled her heart with peace, "How Great Thou Art."

As she sang, she couldn't help but think of Jackson and how she had fallen in love with him in the midst of difficulty and against all wisdom. She'd believed he had feelings for her, too, but their lives were on different tracks and they weren't meant to be.

How great Thou art. But knowing it and being able to accept it were two totally different things. Through all her life, all the trials and tribulations of the past year, her faith hadn't wavered, but now, as she sat here alone, her heart was breaking and loneliness threatened to undermine every belief she had. Her voice faltered.

"I know I'm being tested, Lord. And I'm failing." She was clinging to her faith by her fingernails. "Please, Lord, help me. I know You have a plan for me. Please help me to trust in it. Help me to truly believe that it is Your will, not mine, that matters."

She tried singing again, loudly this time, and before long, she was pouring her entire heart and soul into it. The words purified her soul and helped to clear her mind. With the very act of singing, she poured every ounce of her longing and doubt and belief into the words.

Tears were streaming down her cheeks as she held her face up to the sky, belting the final verse out to the heavens.

Jackson stood at the edge of Callie's yard and watched her sing.

He'd parked the trailer at the end of the drive and led his present along on foot because he wanted to surprise her. He'd tethered the horse to the front porch and had been walking up the steps to knock when he'd heard a back door slam. Instinct kicked in, and he dropped his bags and ran around the side, reaching for a gun he no longer carried.

The sight of Callie alone on her back porch had been so achingly sad, he'd hesitated to interfere. Then she'd walked across the lawn and begun to sing, and he'd been transfixed.

Her song was soft and sad at first, but as she continued, her voice rose with growing passion until it was soaring across the silent morning. When she finished, Jackson almost expected to hear a roar of applause. It was what she deserved. There was total silence instead, as if every ounce of energy had been sucked from the morning by her song. She stood with head bowed.

Slowly, as if sensing something, she turned and saw him. "Jackson?"

He couldn't hear her voice, but he saw her whisper his name. And then she was running toward him, flying across the lawn and leaping into his arms.

The force of her embrace nearly knocked him to his knees, but Jackson swung her up and around, holding her close to his heart. It was a very long time before he drew back enough to see her face.

She lifted her hand to trace along his jaw. "You're really here."

His smile came from the very depths of his being. "I am."

"How—"

"Shh."

He lowered his lips to hers and finally kissed her with all the love in his heart. Love, faith, gratitude, everything in him poured through that kiss as he made up for the long lonely months without her. When he finally lifted his head, they were both gasping for breath.

"What are you doing here? Nothing happened, did it?" She stepped back to look him over.

He laughed. "Nope. Everything's right with the world."

"Really?" Her brow furrowed.

"I brought you a friend. Come meet him." He led Callie over to meet her new horse. "Turns out there was some reward money for helping catch the drug dealers. You have plenty of cash left over to make a new start, but I thought you might like to have a friend along."

She tore her gaze away from her horse to look at him. "You did this, all of this, didn't you? I knew it was more than WITSEC could provide."

He shrugged. "My parents left me a lot of money. I never knew what to do with it. And then I did. I hope it makes you happy."

Her smile faded. She buried her face in the horse's mane. "Can I name him after you—to remind myself?" Her voice was so sad he thought his heart might break.

He waited a beat. "You could, but it might be a bit confusing to know which of us you're calling."

Her head jerked up, startling the horse. She ran a hand over his flank, soothing him as she glared at Jackson. "What exactly are you saying?"

He got down on one knee. "Callie Martin, will you marry me?"

She just stared and for a moment he was afraid he'd made a huge mistake.

"But—" Tears pooled in her eyes. "You'd be giving up so much."

"Oh, sweet girl, I'd be giving up everything if I let you walk out of my life."

Callie stood in shock. "You really mean it? You're not teasing me or trying to get back at me for something I did?"

He laughed. "You really have a low opinion of me."

"Oh, no, that's not what—"

He silenced her with a kiss. "Did that feel like I was teasing?"

She could barely breathe so she shook her head.

He took her hands and linked his fingers through hers. "Callie, when I came home from the war, I joined the Marshals because I had nothing left I cared about. I didn't worry about the danger because I had no reason to live. I figured I might as well do some good with my life."

He lifted her hands and kissed her fingers, one at a time. "You gave me a reason to live. You gave me a life to want. You gave me love and hope at a time when I didn't really expect either."

He closed his eyes and took a long breath. When he opened them again, he stared deep into hers, opening a window into his heart. "Without you, I'm just another marshal. With you, I can be everything.

"I love you, Callie. And I trust you with my whole heart.

"And I'm still waiting on an answer." He laughed nervously. "Will you marry me? Will you let me stay?"

Callie gasped. "Let you stay? How can you? Jackson, what haven't you told me?"

He grinned sheepishly. "That I already left the US Marshals. That God told me He had other plans for me. Plans that included a certain former witness with a love for horses."

Callie's squeal drowned out his words, but he kept talking. "I've spent too many years surrounded by violence, Callie. I want peace. I want to help others heal. How would you like to work with me? I figured we could raise horses and maybe children, and you can do whatever else your heart desires. Maybe take in some foster children, maybe—"

"Oh you lovely, lovely man." She threw herself into his arms. "I love you so much."

From safe within Jackson's embrace, she looked skyward and mouthed the prayer from deep within her heart. *Thank You, thank You, thank You, Lord. Thank You for helping me to trust in Your plan and thank You for giving me Jackson.*

He set her on her feet. "Did you say something?"

She looked up at him. Her smile a mile wide, she winked at him. "Just chatting with God."

"Did He have an answer for me since apparently you don't?"

She nodded.

"Callie?" Jackson growled and lifted her up onto the horse. "I'm not letting you down until you give me the answer I want."

She smiled coyly at him. "It's kind of hard to kiss you from up here."

He shook his head. "Not until you say yes."

She smiled, an expression of such pure joy and love that his heart overflowed. "Well, then let me down and kiss me, Jackson, because my answer is yes. Yes, I will marry you and yes, I will raise horses and children with you, but only if you promise to kiss me every single day for the rest of our lives."

Jackson helped her slide down from the horse and into his arms. When he had her safely caught in his embrace, he closed his eyes and just savored the joy.

Callie reached up and drew his face down to hers. "I love you, Jackson," she whispered as his lips came down across hers. "And I will cherish you every moment of the rest of our lives."

* * * * *

Dear Reader,

Thank you for reading my debut book with Love Inspired Suspense. I hope you enjoyed reading Callie and Jackson's story as much as I enjoyed writing it.

When the editors of Love Inspired Suspense announced the Killer Voices competition in February 2013, I knew I wanted to write a story about an ordinary woman whose life is turned upside down by events beyond her control. Callie's experience is extreme. Fortunately, most of us don't witness murders or events that force us to go on the run. But we all encounter difficulties in our lives. We all face troubles that overwhelm us, that we can't get through on our own. Callie uses her experience to draw closer to the Lord. I hope that through her witness I can inspire others to draw closer to the Lord, to call on Him in times of joy and need.

I used a quote from Isaiah in this story: "For I am the Lord your God who takes hold of your right hand and says to you, Do not fear; I will help you (Isaiah 41:13)."

That verse has been such a comfort to me. The image of God our Father holding on to us, keeping us from despair, is so vivid. I hope it brings you comfort and gives you the strength it gave Callie.

Then there's Jackson. Callie is one lucky lady to have him. I think I fell in love with him the moment he told Callie that her security had been compromised. If you have to go on the run, a marshal like Jackson sure makes it exciting.

I would love to hear from you and know your thoughts about my story. Please visit my website at www.catenolan-author.com to learn more about me and my upcoming books.

Blessings,

Cate

REQUEST YOUR FREE BOOKS!

2 FREE RIVETING INSPIRATIONAL NOVELS
PLUS 2 FREE MYSTERY GIFTS

Love Inspired®
SUSPENSE
RIVETING INSPIRATIONAL ROMANCE

YES! Please send me 2 FREE Love Inspired® Suspense novels and my 2 FREE mystery gifts (gifts are worth about $10). After receiving them, if I don't wish to receive any more books, I can return the shipping statement marked "cancel." If I don't cancel, I will receive 4 brand-new novels every month and be billed just $4.99 per book in the U.S. or $5.49 per book in Canada. That's a savings of at least 17% off the cover price. It's quite a bargain! Shipping and handling is just 50¢ per book in the U.S. and 75¢ per book in Canada.* I understand that accepting the 2 free books and gifts places me under no obligation to buy anything. I can always return a shipment and cancel at any time. Even if I never buy another book, the two free books and gifts are mine to keep forever.

123/323 IDN GH5Z

Name	(PLEASE PRINT)	
Address		Apt. #
City	State/Prov.	Zip/Postal Code

Signature (if under 18, a parent or guardian must sign)

Mail to the **Reader Service:**
IN U.S.A.: P.O. Box 1867, Buffalo, NY 14240-1867
IN CANADA: P.O. Box 609, Fort Erie, Ontario L2A 5X3

**Are you a current subscriber to Love Inspired® Suspense books
and want to receive the larger-print edition?
Call 1-800-873-8635 or visit www.ReaderService.com.**

* Terms and prices subject to change without notice. Prices do not include applicable taxes. Sales tax applicable in N.Y. Canadian residents will be charged applicable taxes. Offer not valid in Quebec. This offer is limited to one order per household. Not valid for current subscribers to Love Inspired Suspense books. All orders subject to credit approval. Credit or debit balances in a customer's account(s) may be offset by any other outstanding balance owed by or to the customer. Please allow 4 to 6 weeks for delivery. Offer available while quantities last.

Your Privacy—The Reader Service is committed to protecting your privacy. Our Privacy Policy is available online at www.ReaderService.com or upon request from the Reader Service.
We make a portion of our mailing list available to reputable third parties that offer products we believe may interest you. If you prefer that we not exchange your name with third parties, or if you wish to clarify or modify your communication preferences, please visit us at www.ReaderService.com/consumerschoice or write to us at Reader Service Preference Service, P.O. Box 9062, Buffalo, NY 14240-9062. Include your complete name and address.

LIS15